Red as Apple

By Steven W. Simon

Fourth Edition, January 2023

ISBN: 979-8-3484-8159-9

boundharepress.com

For Daliah and Nathan.

It was the cicadas on these hot August evenings that elicited childhood dreams in that rural America, Their droning songs in that humidity that never seemed to break. Seaweed green outer shells infused with black to match jet black eyes bugged out. Translucent wings, veiny lines enmeshed throughout at odd angles. Inch-long prehistoric reminders with thick width— perfectly designed for phobic reactions.

Morning brought fear to the cicada itself. The first break of light paralyzed the ones who had not found haven. He pressed against the trees, in the blades. On pavement. On brick. Siding. He prayed that his white underside was hidden from birds swooping and squirrels bounding. The unlucky few were clamped into claws, beaks and canines, and how they screamed. A cicada in peril foretells death for a distance—how they did scream.

1

The night had gone deep towards morning. The cicadas had retreated and the owls retired with their meals earned on the hunt. In the quiet a docile cicada crawled with his thin, black legs up the side of a barn. A barn with only remnants of deep burgundy paint upon wooden boards. Split from the heat, then winter death, then spring rains, and then cycled again for years. He was tranquil in the darkness. Chirped, chirped, then nothing and the night air returned to silent inquiries among the insects.

Moments passed, and in one of those, the guttural rumble of a pickup truck broke through the softness. Headlights set to high beam cut through the darkness. Thick tires disturbed the dirt, crackled as they rolled over the gravel. It traveled down the unpaved road, and then veered right into a driveway of gravel and dirt. Past a dilapidated farmhouse, a rusted fence, miscellaneous farm equipment, disassembled and incomplete, bunched against a storage shed. An orange feral cat ran fast across the lit land in front of the truck as it slowed. Her eyes glowed as she took stock of the noise then bounded over the equipment remnants and disappeared through a gap in the shed. The truck continued, beyond a pen and an abandoned 1967 Chevrolet Impala, metallic blue under rust.

It was a standard cab Ford, late 70s model. Midnight black tinged brown and stripped down to its function. The hood canted forward for perceived aggression. Square headlights separated by a steel grill. It grunted over gravel, before slowing with squelching brakes at a dirt clearing near the cicada's barn. *Click, click, click* into park. A quick ignition turn and the night returned to natural silence.

The man sat stoic in the cab, peering at the barn, illuminated by the headlights. His lips were pursed, his breath steady through his nose. His pale skin and stout features were shadowed by a dense brown beard that settled just above his chest. A thick build, strength built on manual labor that remained even as unemployment and idleness made his gut protrude.

The door squeaked as he pressed it open and stepped to the gravel earth. He closed in on six feet and faded black work boots with thick soles got him there. He wore light blue jeans, dusty and unwashed. A plaid shirt of maroon, blue and white with a pocket per side covered a white tank undershirt. Turning to the truck bed, he closed the cab door, reconnecting to the frame with proper steel acoustics.

Ansel leaned against the truck, reached into his shirt pocket, and pulled out a pack of Marlboro cigarettes. The pack was half empty, and the remaining cigs had shifted to one side of the soft pack. He shook them until a cigarette appeared halfway out, then grasped it with his lips. He took a metallic lighter from his jean pocket and flipped it open. He peered behind the truck and down the path he had driven down to reach the barn. Satisfied that he was alone, he flicked the lighter and his face glowed as he brought it towards the cigarette.

With the ember alight and the Marlboro secure in his lips, he turned his attention to the truck bed. Rusted in spots. Dinged in spots. He rested his elbows against the painted metal that transitioned to the bare steel of the bed interior. A long drag, then an exhale and the ashen gray smoke set into the black under full moonlight.

A final drag, and he exhaled fully, flicking the spent filter into the open gravel. It spun quickly, and the ember stayed firm as it landed. He leaned into the truck bed and slung a black duffel bag over his shoulder, grasped the metal detector by the handle and, with his other hand, took the shovel. *Click. Click,* as Ansel depressed the light switch through the open truck window, and natural darkness returned.

The gravel shifted under his feet as he walked to the barn. An owl sent warnings, but he could not tell if from the dilapidated structure or a nearby tree. His eyes had yet to adjust to the sudden dark, he stopped and waited for his pupils to expand.

The winds shifted as he stood and, in the breeze, flitted the apple trees. Sweet and earthy, and the foliage and fruit produced a distinct aroma—one he knew. At that moment, he was eight years old, pulling a Radio Flyer wagon with all his might down trampled dirt. The sun shone brightly and created a hue of light only felt in memories. He wore overalls, blue and dusty with one knee frayed, exposing his kneecap. A deep yellow t-shirt, sleeves lined with white stripes and an image of an airplane ironed on. He had wanted to be a pilot. An ace, a hero, a commander of massive jet engines.

A young girl sat with her legs crossed inside the wagon, nearest the back. The sun glanced off her pale, freckled skin. Her ginger hair flowed free. Green eyes, a button nose and deep dimples when she smiled. The same blue overalls covered an eggshell shirt patterned with roses. White canvas shoes with rubber runners to protect her toes.

Ahead of her in the wagon sat a boy, the middle of three siblings. His brown hair lay flat around his head, dropping down and covering his ears. Dirt creeped on his cheeks as he squinted in the sunlight, hiding deep blue eyes. He wore no shirt underneath his overalls.

Apples as red as the wagon itself piled up around the two riders. They bounced around them as the hard rubber wheels traversed the uneven ground while he pulled with all his strength. They tried to ride without holding on, but every time they grabbed the side giggles rang out into the eternity of the farm. As apples fell into their laps, they burst with pain then laughter.

He pulled, and pulled, and cleared the gravel, and the wagon smoothed over thick, green grass, content from summer rains. Exhausted, he slowed and then stopped. The two younger siblings climbed out, each holding several apples. Amanda handed one to Keenan, and then one to him, and they all sat down onto the grass.

The apples crunched with every bite, and juices ran down the children's chins. And when finished, they threw the cores in the direction of a barn—gigantic to their childish perception, freshly painted and unbelievably red.

In that moment, as his eyes adjusted to the darkness, there was no want. No fighting from the master bedroom. No children's teases over matching overalls and worn shoes. No fears of father's belt. No running from mother's wooden spoons in the kitchen. No hunger or cold fingers in winter's depth. There were only apples, sweet and ripe and everything.

A quick shiver broke the moment, and in the moonlight, Ansel approached the barn doors. Ajar and untended, the opening offered enough space for him to squeeze through, pushing the wooden door wider along a rusty track with his back, feet dug into the dirt.

The moonlight filtered through slats in the roof—some pieces had fallen to the floor, enabling the moon further. Three wooden beams descended from the high ceiling, equally spaced along the length of the barn. The last of which anchored to a loft that ran its wooden base to the eastern wall, with a ladder still providing access. Hay bales towered high, although a few had fallen to the ground below, an opportunity for the rodents and, in turn, the cats.

In a corner, under a large opening in the roof where the moonlight flooded in, he set down the metal detector and shovel and unzipped the black duffel bag. He staged the items on the barn floor.

One pair of Koss PRO4AA headphones. Over-ear design, beige shell with black interior.

One Remington 870 Wingmaster 12-gauge shotgun. The stock and pump action, wood—rich and lacquered deep. The body, matte black. Loaded.

One red rectangular Coleman flashlight.

Flashlight in hand, and directed at the floor, he inserted the headphone cord into the detector jack and turned on the machine. In a second the signal flew to the right of the dial, and the tone pierced his ears.

"Fuck!" he yelled as he threw off the headphones and noticed that the wooden shovel was directly below the device. Setting down the detector, he walked the shovel to the wall nearest him and propped it up.

Headphones fitted once again, he grasped the detector and studied the knobs. They were foreign to him, so he let them be. Starting opposite the loft, his right arm swayed, the white underbelly of the machine a few inches from the ground. Steady in its alert, close in his ears. The flashlight secured in his left hand, revealing only that which mattered in the moment.

At the first beam the alert heightened. He paused, studied the rusted metal bolts at the base, and continued. Slow progress as he focused. To the middle beam, and then under the loft. *Beep.* Pause. *Beep.* Pause. *Beep.* Back to center, then near where he had started. *Beep.* Pause. *Beep.* Pause. *Beep.* Again, he turned. Again, he paced. Through the spilt hay under the loft. *Beep.* *Beep.* *Beep.* *Beep.* *Beep.* *Beep.* He stopped.

He slid the hay from under him with his foot to make a clearing, then crouched down and drew an 'x' with his finger. Off with the headphones, detached from the detector, he grabbed the shovel and set the flashlight down, creating horizontal light to the 'x.' With a heft, he drove the shovel into the dirt crust, fogging the halo of light in dust undisturbed for many a year.

2

It takes a certain kind of man to drive the all-new 1986 Mercedes-Benz 560 SL. Sophisticated. Powerful. Mysterious, yet confident. Women turn their heads as he steps out and walks confidently to the office. Men of less stature nod with respect for his prowess, his desire.

The interior—roomy, sumptuously comfortable with modern appointments. He can be sure a woman swoons upon her entrance. The elegance that surrounds her subconsciously transfers to him. His elegance. His sophistication. She yearns. She wants. She is yours.

Keenan Butler drove carefully on this country road, as he did on all uneven and rough thoroughfares. 'It is required to respect such a vehicle, as others are obliged to respect such a man who would own such an enviable machine,' he had thought on many occasions, in one form or another. Out here, he had forgotten how thick the night was in the rural expanse. The mechanisms of man soothed no one here at this hour, as they were conspicuous in their absence to those who knew them.

Clean shaven, save for a dense, coffee-colored mustache. His hair neatly combed, parted to the right and tight with mousse setting just over his ears. Fair skin concealed by tanning beds. Shallow-set blue eyes hidden by gold rimmed glasses, set large about his nose. He wore a white silk shirt, short sleeved, underneath a gray vest. Khaki pants flared at his thighs and cinnamon boat shoes accented with beige stitching. Argyle socks peeked through as he controlled the pedals.

His destination was far enough off the road to be invisible, and so he drove from memory. A mile out at 'willow tree arch.' Half mile at 'three rocks.' Quarter mile from 'children crossing.' And a hundred yards after the dip he slowed and searched for a solitary driveway on his right.

The sedan crept up the drive, crunching the gravel as it compressed, then released. Veered to the right of a farmhouse and miscellaneous farm equipment, abandoned and strewn among a shed. Beyond an old Chevy and to a clearing.

Keenan slowed the car as he drove, then parked next to the Ford pickup truck. The car went silent, and he pulled the handle and swung the door open. Stepping out, he felt the summer heat that had not dissipated with the sunset. He ran a hand over his bushy mustache, pressing it down, and then releasing the hand at his chin. In front of him a barn, and while he had remembered the place, being there brought memories that had been hidden for years.

The lights from Keenan's car pierced the decaying slats and the open door. Ansel shut off the flashlight. He Ignored the shovel for the shotgun, positioned himself against the agape door, and gained the nerve to peer into the peripheral darkness with only his head exposed to the clearing. His vision was acclimated to the night, although the headlights blinded him to any figure. His heart magnified in his ears. The barrel lowered, sliding against the frayed wood of the door as it leveled. His heart rate steadied, and with it, his breathing slowed but remained deep. The shotgun gently rose with every inhale, gently fell with every exhale. He cocked the hammer as a shadow blocked one headlight, then the other.

"Ansel," Keenan said in a strong whisper. "Ansel, are you in there?"

Ansel kept the gun pointed outward. The figure took shape in the open space between the headlight and the barn door.

"Ansel?" he said again, this time louder.

"This is my friend," Ansel said in a murmur to himself, his lips barely moving and hidden under his beard. The gun still aimed, still cocked. His mind maneuvered as it battled the finger pressed against the trigger. "This is my friend. This is my brother."

"Goddammit, Ansel!" Keenan screamed quietly. "Your boy said you're here. Your truck is here for Christ's sake."

"This is my friend. This is my brother," Ansel muttered, and slowly his breathing settled and his mind returned. He pushed the hammers forward and lowered the gun. He stepped from behind the door and walked several paces into the clearing. Keenan stepped forward and met him in the halogen halo, careful to pick his feet up properly as to not scuff the leather of his shoes.

The two men stood in the halogen halo created by the headlights. Ansel studied Keenan's pressed shirt and pleated pants. Keenan, Ansel's grungy outfit and the shotgun. It was Keenan who took the first step forward, and the two brothers embraced.

"Good to see you, Ansel," Keenan said while patting him on the back.

"Yeah, you too."

"Been too long."

They separated, and Keenan stepped back, but still stared at his brother. Ansel took the soft pack of Marlboros from his plaid pocket and shook it until a filter stuck out from the open end. He extended one towards Keenan, who took one between his thumb and forefinger. Another shake, and Ansel took one himself.

"We agreed tomorrow," Keenan said through a smoky exhale.

"I couldn't wait."

"Amanda is going to be pissed."

"Yeah."

They both pivoted and stared at the barn as they smoked.

"Thought the next time I'd be around here would be for a funeral," Keenan said to the barn.

"He's alright."

"Real skinny though."

"He's comin' 'round."

Keenan dropped his cigarette and crushed the butt with the sole of his shoe. Ansel followed suit. They walked to the barn. Both excited, both hesitant. The owl made himself known. The cicada, scarce.

The shovel remained fast in the dirt, a demarcation to their prize. Ansel crouched, pressed on the flashlight, setting a mouse scurrying. As he rose, Keenan held out the shovel.

"What?" asked Ansel.

"Here's the shovel," Keenan responded, pushing it forward a few inches.

"You're holding it, you dig."

"Look at what I'm wearing."

"You look, you look, pretty, I guess."

"So what, I'm not getting dirty."

"You should've changed."

"I would have if someone would have waited until tomorrow."

"I ain't shovelin'."

"If I didn't show up, you'd have to shovel."

The younger had a point, and Ansel reluctantly took the shovel. Keenan stepped back, sure that dust would settle on him.

"I'd beat the shit outta you if you weren't wearing that queer shirt."

"I'd whoop your ass, Ansel," Keenan blustered.

Ansel looked up at his brother, sighed, then struck the shovel into the dirt. He dug with accuracy. Repetition. Plaid shirt. Rusted metal against the earth. Worn work boots. He levered horizontally. He raised, turned and shoveled over into the pile under construction. Again, as Keenan stood off to the side, and watched progress in pleated pants, leather boat shoes.

Dried earth continued to reveal itself at one foot. At two feet. At three, the men started to wonder. There was a glance.

"Are you sure this is the right place?"

"It went off," Ansel replied, and took a quick glance at the contraption before continuing to dig.

Keenan stepped closer and crouched down to the metal detector. He looked it over. "This yours?"

"Neighbor's."

"You know how to use it?"

"Enough."

"Enough?"

"It went beep, beep, then it went beep beep beep beep."

Keenan stood, then stepped back to safety as Ansel kept shoveling. At three and a half feet, as measured by the human eye, Keenan wandered. At four, he wondered as he inspected the beams. The walls. Strewn hay. The ladder leading to the loft, and how many times his hands had grasped the smooth wood in anticipation. In fear. In silence and in drunken release.

3

When the weather had warmed, and the frost became memory in the rural expanse, the three siblings would avoid the school bus in favor of walks home. With backpacks slung over their young shoulders, in solidarity amongst the reeds and tall grass awakening beside the roads. The jaunts would settle two hours, three in proper leisure.

Through constant nagging, the occasional beating, and born of embarrassment brought on by classmates, the three no longer wore the matching outfits of their younger days. Although humiliation never quite absolved, as the clothes were found at secondhand outlets, and on some dark days they arrived in outfits formerly worn by their peers.

Ansel, the oldest, always led. He had almost finished his first year of high school, therefore had absolute authority. Keenan and Amanda, both still in junior high, walked together. They were closer in age and fought rarely without Ansel's involvement.

In this connection, deep along a road and fields planted anew against the horizon, Keenan confided in Amanda his first real crush. In return, she giggled, and began to skip around him, her backpack lifting off her shoulders then dropping back down.

"Keenan likes Heather! Keenan likes Heather!"

His cheeks flushed red as he grasped for her dress, but she escaped.

"Keenan *loves* Heather! Keenan *loves* Heather!"

"Shut up!"

"Keenan *loves* Heather! Keenan *loves* Heather!"

"Shut up!"

"I'm gonna tell!"

"No, you're not!"

"Yes, I am!"

She continued with smirks and kissy faces the remainder of the walk. Once inside the house, Keenan bounded up the stairs for his bedroom and stayed locked away through dinner.

The next day, inverted on the monkey bars at recess, Amanda did tell. Everyone within earshot.

"Keenan loves Heather! Keenan loves Heather!"

All the while, Keenan hid in a concrete tunnel, nearest the swings. His head tucked between his knees, glasses pressed hard into his brow. He wished hard to stay there forever, to never come out of that concrete cocoon. Slowly wither and die into nothing. Or, he wished less dramatically, to be in his bedroom, tightly wrapped in blankets. Head pushed deep into the mattress and overlaid with pillows.

As the final bell rang, he shoved his books into his backpack and ran down the hall. He remembered Mr. Schneider yelling at him to stop running, but he didn't. Out the front doors, beyond the bus where Heather would surely board, and towards home he ran. Anger at Amanda. Anger at imagined denial from Heather. At his used Nikes for not getting him home fast enough. At teachers for his grades. At everything. Everything.

In the morning, he feigned sickness. Under threat, he reluctantly dressed for school. Under threat, he walked to the back of the bus and sat where the cool kids, the bullies had dibs. And when they pressed him on the trespass, he simply stared ahead, unfocused, into an imagined void where they could not see him. In youth, trepidation transposed effortlessly, and they gave him a pass.

At recess he bolted for the safety of the tunnel. Tucked fetal. Duck. Cover. He listened to his breath, the muted resonances of play. Of juvenile conversations and negotiations. Of tag. Of kickball. Of balls bouncing off metal rims. And then a voice less muted, one he thought to be unreal, if he had not smelled the lavender and lilac. Meek, supernaturally sweet.

"Hey," said the voice.

Keenan pushed deeper into himself. He imagined again being in his bed, under layers of blankets, and he tried desperately to will her away.

"Hey," again.

Steadily, awkwardly, he lifted his head off his knees and turned toward the voice. Quite convinced he had prayed hard enough in the interim that she would not notice the dread in his eyes. The minute beads of sweat bordering his nose, under thick eyeglass frames. The tremor in his hands as he produced a feigned smile, his lips still tight.

"Hey," Keenan replied, hoping that his voice would not crack. It held.

Heather had sat down opposite him in the playground tunnel. A few feet separated them along the length of the tube. She plucked a dandelion that had sprouted through cracks in the edifice and twirled it between her fingers.

Cinnamon hair curled down her neck and settled below her shoulders. An emerald barrette to each side, framing her soft, freckled face. Her skin taught, slender, yet ample her youthful features. Brown eyes set perfectly that beckoned every boy. A slender nose, pouty lips.

She wore a plaid dress that led with hunter green, complemented by black and white. Ivory white short sleeves that puffed out around her arm. An ivory white collar. Starched. Ironed. White socks under black shoes, leather straps tight over her feet and connected with a metal snap.

"Mama says these are weeds," Heather said, studying the dandelion, "looks like a flower to me."

"They're weeds, I think," said Keenan.

She stared at it, and he mimicked, which gave him a respite from her features.

"Amanda says you got horses. You got horses?"

"Nah," he said, staring at the concrete, "she's fibbing."

"Oh."

Heather shifted her feet as Keenan sat silent. His heart thumped before every word, and gave him pause.

"But we got other things. Like chickens, and a couple goats right now. Supposed to get some cows but not till later."

Heather listened, then her attention drifted out the tunnel.

"But we got kittens too," Keenan added.

"I love kittens!" As a smile parted her lips.

"Do you, um," Keenan started, looking away with the fear of rejection tightly held, "You wanna come, you wanna come over and see, I mean you could pet them. If you want. Sometime."

Heather jumped to her feet, crouched over to avoid the tunnel ceiling. She shuffled her feet to the opening and stepped out into the grass. She turned back to face Keenan, who watched her with sweaty palms, fists clenched.

"I would love to pet your kittens sometime, Keenan Butler," and she immediately broke into giggles, then ran off.

◆ ◆ ◆

Steel against earth. Scrape. Grunt. Falling dirt. It had become a song to the brothers. Although the coda had not been determined, they felt it was near. Sweat dripped from Ansel's forehead. His arms ached. He pined for a cigarette.

Steel. Earth. Scrape. Grunt. Fall. Keenan paced, careful in his step. Even as he moved, he seemed relaxed, having nowhere to be and doing none of the work. Steel against metal.

Ansel dug into the dirt, and something metallic rung out and reverberated off the barn walls. Ansel drove the shovel down again, just to make sure. Metal. Keenan hurried over, grabbed the flashlight, and crouched at the hole's edge. Ansel found the edges and carved out the rectangular shape abutting its borders.

Once sufficient, he laid the shovel atop the hay. He went to his knees, then bent over the opening. His belly, under plaid, flattened out against the ground. He brushed loose dirt from the object and, grabbing the handle, extracted it from the earth. He set it down gingerly upon the hay.

The toolbox was painted black, nicked and scratched here and there revealing the steel construction. Three feet long. Nine, maybe ten inches both wide and deep. Two hinged latches, left and right of center, and dirt remained in the steel curves. Ansel lifted a latch, it clicked and the settled dirt fell. He reached for the second.

"Wait," Keenan said, jolting the silence.

Ansel froze in place, his eyes remained fixated on the latch.

"We have to wait for Amanda."

Ansel's hand was still mid-reach for the latch, then relaxed.

"We can jus' look now, it makes no difference," Ansel replied.

"No. Has to be all of us."

"We can act surprised, as if we didn't look."

Keenan thought on it. "No, you'd mess it up."

Ansel tensed. He readied a response, but only a melancholy sigh escaped. It was Amanda, he remembered, who had understood the toolbox. He flipped the open latch down, then stood with it in hand. Keenan followed it with the flashlight, then collected the metal detector and shovel. They stood next to each other in the muted light.

"It's good to see you again, Ansel."

"Yeah," said Ansel, after a pause, then started out of the barn.

Keenan placed the shovel and detector in the truck bed, then turned off the flashlight and set it with the tools. Ansel hefted the toolbox to the bed.

"Put it in the cab," Keenan said.

Ansel hesitated, then lifted the box out and walked to the passenger door.

"You need a place?" Ansel asked, opening the door.

"No, staying at a hotel."

Ansel shut the door with a thud, a clunk. He took a cigarette from the pack and gave one to Keenan.

"Nice place," Keenan continued exhaling smoke into the dank air, "quite a ways from here but worth it. Room service. King size bed. Fancy sheets and pretty girls working the front desk."

"Sounds nice."

"Mini bar. Breakfast with bacon and omelets." Keenan took his last drag and dropped the cigarette. He stepped toward Ansel and set his arm on his shoulder.

"I trust you, Ansel," he said, looking into his eyes and squeezing the damp shoulder. "We'll open it tomorrow. Me, you and Amanda."

4

The Keyes Motel was a survivor, a descendent of the New Deal. Visible from the interstate, it touted air conditioning and in-room telephones. Adjacent to, and across a frontage road from a truck stop, it offered hourly, nightly, and weekly accommodations. 'Vacancy' blazed in red neon below the sign spelling out the motel name in blue cursive letters set against rusted white paint.

The office was clad in wood paneling, designed to imitate oak yet never achieving that purpose. Softly lit by the few ceiling lights operational, and a burnt orange table lamp set in a corner. A burgundy loveseat, armrests worn and stained. Black plastic ashtray upon a glass top coffee table.

The man stood patiently and welcoming behind the counter, which was unexpected and unwarranted at this hour. He was tall and thin, with intense features pronounced on a clean-shaven face with warm ivory tones. Wrinkled, yet taut. Narrow lips, pursed except in conversation. His eyes a penetrating mocha, set in, for he was on in age.

He wore a crimson robe, accented with gray stripes at the wrists. A white undershirt. Around his neck a leather strap, and from it dangled a pair of reading glasses.

"I'd like a room, please," said Keenan.

"Of course, sir," the motel manager said, "I will need to see identification, please."

Keenan reached into his pocket and handed over his driver's license. The manager grasped it gently, then set it down on his side of the counter. He set the reading glasses upon the tip of his nose, then began filling out a form attached to a clipboard.

"Welcome, Mr. Butler," the manager said with eye contact, then returned to the form. "And how long will you be staying with us?"

"A few days."

"Is that three, then?"

"Three is good," Keenan said, unsure in his voice.

"Very good, sir." The manager looked up for a moment, then returned to the form.

"New York City," the manager said, "quite a ways. Are you here on business, if you don't mind me asking?"

"I am," Keenan responded after a pause.

"Get a few salesmen that come through this way, not so much anymore," the manager responded as he filled out the form and handed back Keenan's identification. "Will you need use of the telephone?"

"How much is that?"

"Fifty cents per night for unlimited local calls."

"No, thank you."

The manager finished with the form and set the clipboard on the counter.

"Here is the room costs," he said, pointing with the pen, "Comes to eighty-six dollars."

Room 7. Wallpapered walls that failed to mask the movement and voices from adjoining rooms. Beige, pink flowers faded and peeling at the corners. A queen size mattress. Stiff. Decorated with a thin comforter, patterned with brown and yellow

and orange. Two limp pillows cased in white. A small wood table that wobbled, set below the open window adjacent to the door. Two chairs, one that matched the table, the other with a metal frame and taupe cushions.

A Winston burned in the black ashtray on the end table, lit softly by a lamp. An open pack, a few cans of beer, and a plastic container with half a ham and cheese sandwich.

Keenan lay on the bed in his t-shirt and underwear and sipped a Budweiser. His clothes from the day set upon a dresser. Over the echo of a woman's orgasm, a man's animalistic grunts beyond the walls, he thought about failures past. Imagined their end, settling into the fiefdom of soft memories. Depleted, only rushing forward with focused intent. He had stopped imagining himself a man of money, of power, until that phone call from Amanda. He daydreamed and hoped he would not make the same mistakes again, though doubt pressed. For those who go all-in, there are destined many who fall flat. Ruthless were the traders on Wall Street, and Keenan could only pretend for so long. They saw weakness and pounced. Pounced with the façade of friendship that mirrored psychopathy. Pounced with prostitutes, champagne and cocaine. He was smitten even in complete loss and utter betrayal and vowed to return as a successful psychopath as soon as possible. It was the antithesis of earlier memories that beckoned him. That sweet nectar of hope.

Moving beyond the unending concrete, he returned in a vibrant memory to the barn. He grasped the bottom rung of the loft ladder and started to ascend. He climbed quickly, not wanting to give Heather the opportunity to study his attire. He turned and peered over the edge. Her auburn hair was split into two ponytails. Eyes glinted in the slatted sunshine. She wore a powder blue dress, white, knee-high socks and pink shoes with little bows atop.

"C'mon, it's not that high up."

She reached for a rung, then hesitated.

"I'm a little scared. What if I fall?"

"You ain't gonna fall. Besides, this is where the kittens are, so if you want to see 'em."

She looked left, then right, and started to climb.

"See, it's easy."

Heather reached the straw strewn floor of the loft. Keenan reached out his hand and pulled her up. She crawled away from the ladder to the haven of the loft's center. In the corner, amongst the bales of hay a litter of kittens slept, away from the penetrating light that lit specks of dust and hay in the air. Gray and brown, hinting at orange around their faces. Aligned, whiskers pressed against their mother.

She reached tentatively and touched gingerly, not wanting to wake them. Ran her fingers along their backs and explored the soft sensations and gentle purrs. Keenan picked one up and cradled it in the crook of his arm. The mother raised her eyes to him, then returned to slumber.

"This one's my favorite."

"Why's that?"

"Cause he follows me around, talking to me."

"Did you name him?"

"Burp."

"What?"

"His name is Burp."

"That's a stupid name for a cat."

"Well what would you name him?"

"I would name him Henry."

"That's a person's name."

"It's proper, and I like it."

"He's my cat, and he's Burp," Keenan said forcefully. Heather shuffled in the hay and turned her attention to the floorboards.

"But you can name any other cat," Keenan continued, "a proper cat's name."

Heather ignored him. Keenan put Burp back in the litter, then grabbed another. He shuffled over to her and lightly set it in her lap. She put out her arms to cradle it.

"You want this one to be Henry?"

"Is it a boy or a girl?"

"I don't know."

"Let's pretend it's a girl."

"Okay."

"Hmmm. I think... How about Elizabeth, like the queen?"

"What queen?"

"The queen of England, Keenan."

Keenan knew nothing of this queen, nor England, and said nothing. He found the conversation uncomfortable and instead considered her cinnamon locks as they crested upon her shoulders. Her eyes as she looked at the content kitten, wrapped in her freckled arms.

"She's purring," Heather said excitedly, "I can feel it." Looking up at him, she began to smile, though Keenan did not see it. He had closed his eyes, pursed his lips and leaned into her. Hands pressed into the hay, prickling his skin. He leaned in. Closer. Closer, and where he had expected her lips to meet his there was nothing. His eyes shot open to see her compressed against the wooden slats of the wall, her feet still pushing backwards and away. The kitten struggled to get her bearings in the straw, having been roused from such a slumber. Heather's arms were draped around her knees, red from wood and straw. "I don't kiss poor boys, Keenan," her eyes hidden, "I just wanted to see your kittens."

The adjacent motel room had gone quiet for several minutes, then Keenan heard the door open, then shut. From the open window he watched an obese man amble across the parking lot, silhouetted by intermittent lights in the lot, the rows of lights lining the motel doors. He climbed into a rig at the truck stop. Another sip, another drag, then a crushed cigarette in the ashtray. He turned off the lamp and willed himself to sleep.

5

Ansel's sunken eyes strained against the dim kitchen lamp overhead. He had tossed in slumber and gave up in the pre-dawn aura to the birds roused and vocal. Clad in an old green t-shirt with white screen-printed text ;Northern Trucking,' dirty jeans, his eyes were upon the toolbox, set upon the table amid the chaos of random dishes. Envelopes postmarked and left unopened. Sports pages. Classifieds circled in blue ink. Truck driver. Forklift operator. General help. All relegated to the table's edge, cluttered countertops.

The toolbox seemed less impressive to him in the flooded light as opposed to the sharp focus of the flashlight. Dents popped. Rusted surfaces became real to the touch. Although the latches retained their metallic sheen as if polished by their subterranean resting place. He ran his fingers over the left latch, feeling the smooth edge that canted out. Placed his forefinger underneath and lifted. The latch clicked, unnaturally loud in the stillness. He looked up at his son,

Daniel, for movement, still slumbering on the couch.

Ansel stared at the couch, its faded jade faux leather cracked at the armrests, set near the center of the living room, and imagined real leather. It faced the wall with a television set on a dark stained cabinet, and its back created a path between the wall to the front door. Daniel didn't stir, and Ansel turned his eyes to the toolbox.

Ansel guided the right latch open, muted, unlike the click of the former. He grasped the corners of the lid and pushed it open. He breathed slowly, methodically through his nose as he processed the sight. He had believed he was cursed. That, despite all efforts, all trials would end in stagnation at best. He was cursed, and his indifference to superstition or religion meant that there was no plausible way to lift it spiritually. That maybe, just maybe, if he persevered long enough, a tangible fork in the road would break it, and remove the echoing sorrow. Hardship. In front of his eyes was the egress. Here was hope, palpable and perceptible. Here was hope, and he didn't know how to process it. All he knew was that action was needed. Now.

The bedroom closet was filled haphazardly with clothes, cardboard boxes, and arbitrary items of varying sentimentality. Ansel rifled through the mess and grabbed a flower-printed suitcase from the corner recess. He placed it on the unkept bed and unzipped the cover. Took out folded woman's clothes and placed them reverently back in the closet. Quickly to the dresser he stepped around dirty clothes, and chose an assortment of apparel, filling half the suitcase.

Daniel's room matched the disarray found throughout the home. A Hulk Hogan poster was taped to the wall nearest the window. Macho Man Randy Savage above the dresser, above WWF action figures settled among Star Wars. Luke Skywalker. Han Solo. An x-wing fighter. Settled among He-Man figures with battle-scar actions. Settled among pill bottles. Asparaginase. Cyclophosphamide. Cytarabine.

The sun had started to crest over the flat expanse as Ansel shoved open the screen door and behind him it sprung shut. He dragged the suitcase over unmown grass intertwined with weeds. Beyond the aged oak, a frayed rope hung from a branch to a car tire. He hefted the luggage into the truck bed.

Swiftly back to the kitchen table. Reverence where reverence was due, he stood over the toolbox before closing the lid and replacing the latches. Clutching the handle firmly, he walked past the couch, grabbed the Remington, and shot out the door. The commotion had roused Daniel, and he watched his father's movements, his knees on the couch and his head peeking out over the back of the couch.

There was deep awareness behind his eyes, deep sable lenses that almost disappeared into his pupils. Ashen skin, smooth, that matched a child younger than his seven years. Subtle blonde eyebrows and peach fuzz hair that disappeared in certain light, making the tops of his ears appear to stick out. His t-shirt was loose over his frail frame, white with red at the collar, the sleeves. He-Man, with ripped muscles and yellow hair, ironed on the front.

Ansel dropped the toolbox and gun in the truck bed, took several steps back to the house, then stopped in mid stride. He stared at the front door, then turned to stare at the truck. He walked back, took the toolbox out of the bed and placed it in the cab. As he locked the doors he tried to remember the last time he had a need to secure the vehicle.

Daniel took a glass from the kitchen counter, poured out the remaining water, and filled it up in the sink. Shutting off the tap, he drank thirstily, then returned the cup to the sink for another fill.

"What's going on?" he asked his father who came through the front door.

"Nothing," Ansel responded. He looked for something more to distract his mind but found nothing.

"What's in the toolbox?"

"Ain't your business."

"Where's my medicine?"

"I got 'em."

"Where?"

"Just let me think for a minute!"

Ansel found his cigarettes on the counter and lit one with a match, shook it, then set the blackened head in an overflowing glass ashtray. Daniel left the kitchen and turned on the television in the living room. He pressed the power button on the Nintendo and Super Mario Bros. flashed on the screen.

Ansel rested his elbows on the counter that divided the kitchen and living room. Through the smoke, he took in the smallness of his surroundings. The dilapidation kept up only to the point of habitation. It had been some time since he took stock, as the blinders of despair are thorough in their manipulations.

The burgundy carpet was discolored here, there. Wood panels had come unglued and bulged. The couch was hardened by a decade of setting suns. The window screen was unsealed at two of four corners. The spackled drywall from where he punched through when desperation became too great, and covered hastily when he had recovered and felt the embarrassment. In hope he could take stock, he could face the flaws. In hope he could see in it a past. In hope, he could imagine burning it all down and running out the door.

His instinct was to run. He wanted to run. Yet he had no comprehension of a life outside this town or the next one over. Outside of here he would be an outsider, recognized as such within seconds. He was an outsider here, sure, but one that was accepted. City names ran through his mind. The closer he got to the coasts, the more he hesitated.

The reality of running extinguished with his cigarette, and he walked with slumped shoulders to the truck and turned the key. He brought the toolbox back into the house and slid it under his bed. He brought the Remington back and set it near the door. He brought the suitcase back and took out the pill bottles and set them next to the kitchen sink.

"Finish up your game and get dressed," Ansel said, entering the kitchen from the bedroom.

"I just started."

"Don't matter."

"Where we going?"

"Breakfast. We're gonna go get some breakfast."

"Don't I have to take my medicine?"

"Well, yeah."

"Probably gonna barf it all up if I do."

"Tell you what," Ansel said, "les' wait until after and you can take it then."

◆ ◆ ◆

Uncle Joe's Family Restaurant was set along a sparse main street not planned for leisurely shopping or congregation. Set near a gas station, a used car lot, a hardware store, a bar and a health clinic. A large sign, white with "restaurant" written in black block letters represented the type of business, yet not which one. A carport, painted beige, ran the length of the parking lot, and led to the main entrance and the building which matched the carport hue. The exterior of the building lacked any charm, nor did it need to at the time it was built. Large windows to the right of the entrance bathed the dining room in sunlight and continued halfway around the side of the building. Inside, booths with light brown cushions lined the walls. Lamps hung above them, molded to resemble old-fashioned lanterns, yet with bulbs. Wooden tables, stained dark, filled out the middle, adorned with condiments and napkins. Near the center of the room, a counter reached out from the kitchen door. There were white mugs printed with 'Uncle Joe's' in blue were set upside down on saucers, and where they were righted, gruff men sipped black coffee and ate eggs. Steak. Bacon. Hash browns. Some conversed, others had heads down in newspapers. Some smoked. One flirted with the counter waitress named Mary who had a pencil tucked in her wild red hair and a large bosom and wide rear end.

"I want pancakes," began Daniel to the waitress. She was young, with a thickness found in most farm girls. Blonde hair pulled into a ponytail. A cute, stout face with full lips that parted slowly when she spoke and chewed gum when listening.

"Start over," Ansel said sternly without looking up from the spoon swirling slowly in his coffee.

"May I have pancakes with sausage please?" Daniel said, looking at his father for approval, but received no signal.

"Alright sweetie, what to drink?"

"Milk, please."

Ansel sipped his coffee and pressed on one end of a black plastic ashtray with his forefinger, sliding it back and forth across the booth table. Still dressed in He-Man, now blue jeans and a red cap with the Ford logo, Daniel unwrapped his silverware from a napkin, then rolled them back up.

Running creeped back into Ansel's mind, then passed. Returned, and he shuttered to exorcise the thought. He needed what was in the toolbox, all of it. Yet his conscience held firm, and overrode Keenan's fancy car, Amanda's white-picket-perfect Church on Sunday's nuclear family postcard. A third of the money was his, and there was no sense in waiting to have it.

The food arrived, and Daniel set to buttering and smothering his pancakes in syrup, making sure to coat the sausage. He ate with ferocity and had finished before Ansel had even put a dent in his eggs and bacon. Daniel eyed the bacon as he gulped down his milk.

"Still hungry?"

"Very much so."

Ansel smiled, then stroked his beard slowly to hide the emotion. It had been some time since Daniel had an appetite, and it had been years since they had been at a restaurant. He called the waitress over and ordered more pancakes and a side of bacon.

The boy spread butter on pancakes. The waitress topped off coffee. The man drank in between cigarette puffs and thought about purchasing a newspaper without purpose, without flipping past the baseball standings.

◆ ◆ ◆

Daniel slumped down on the bench seat in the truck cab. His belly was full, his eyes drowsy and barely open, hidden from the morning sun. The truck idled in the parking lot of Northwest Community Bank, the engine growling and audible through the open windows. A manicured lawn replete with flower beds lining the walkway that led to two white columns then to glass-paned doors. A red brick exterior with large window panes with outlines that matched the columns. 'Now open on Saturdays 9AM to 1PM,' read the sign dug into the ground nearest the road. Across the street was Eddy's Auto Repair shop. Eddy was often grease-stained, plaid adorned, and unshaven. He spit into the garbage bins set between auto bays and cussed with regularity. Ansel imagined himself there as he pulled open the door, swearing in comfort and spitting if necessary.

The open hall struck Ansel, as it differed greatly from the intimacy of his home, of Uncle Joe's. The repetitive click of dress shoes, heels, echoed and permeated beyond his hearing. With it, he stopped, unsure of his next movement. To his left, a counter of oak, separated into stalls, behind which stood a woman writing something in a ledger. Here, he had deposited government checks and small bills earned from odd jobs. To his right, three oak desks. Each empty except the middle one, where an obese man with an uncooperative comb-over sat typing into a computer, ill-fitted in his suit. A young couple sat across from him, anxious to hear what he would say when he finished typing.

There was unease as Ansel stood a few steps interior. Out of place in plaid and dusty work boots. Conspicuous with a paper grocery bag folded over several times and tucked under his arm. He felt for the first time the dirt and sweat that had accumulated the evening before and he spied his fingertips and the dirt formed under them. He cursed himself for not taking the time to shower as he tightened his grip on the bag, and his nails created indentations in the paper as he turned to leave. Embarrassed. Out of place. Unsure.

"Hello, Mr. Butler!" the teller said, accentuating her voice across the chasm, reverberating throughout. Ansel paused, considered his options and quickly realized he had only one. There were ten banking stalls, hers being nearest the back of the room. He feigned a smile and produced an awkward wave. She waved in kind, exuberantly, as he approached.

"So excited to have a customer," she beamed, "we've been open on Saturdays for nearly a month and I swear I've had maybe five customers." She cleared away the register as Ansel arrived at the stall. "I mean, I know it's for the customer's convenience but," she let out a derisive huff, "I mean there's no customers. Look!"

Ansel politely looked around. There was the couple and the fat man in the suit. He delayed returning to her, as he lacked the ability to match her tone or facial expressions. She was in her late thirties, eyelashes long and deep, contrasting with ruby red lips. Silver hoop earrings, almost ostentatiously large. A thin frame in soft skin, covered with a ruffled pink blouse and navy-blue pencil skirt. Her brunette hair levitated from hairspray in a pristine wave and down to her shoulders.

"Anyways, what can I do for you today, Mr. Butler?"

"I'd like to," he stopped to clear his throat and imagined how she knew him. "I'd like to make a deposit please."

"Of course, do you have your bank book with you?"

"No," he said, looking away at the counter.

"No problem, if I can have your driver's license I can look it up."

Ansel reached into his back pocket and handed the license to her. She took it with a smile and grasped her reading glasses that hung from a beaded chain set against her blouse.

"How's Daniel doing?" she asked, without looking away from the green computer text.

"Daniel?"

"Yes, your son?"

Ansel stared at her.

"Oh I'm so sorry," she said, taking her eyes from the screen. "I'm Mary Baker," she paused, awaiting recognition. "Michael's mother?" another pause. "Has Daniel never spoken about Michael?"

"Oh Michael, yes. Yes. He has."

"Phew, I was beginning to think I had the wrong Mr. Butler, like there's two of you, or I was going crazy or something! Well anyways, I'm head of the PTA at school and we've been trying to get ahold of you. We want to plan something for Daniel and I was hoping you'd stop in cause I'd done banking for you before and here you are!"

"Plan something?"

"Oh you know," she said, now back to the screen, "perhaps a fundraiser or something. You know, get the whole school involved, maybe get Channel 5 to come video it. I've seen them do it on the news plenty of times."

Ansel left her eyes and examined the counter. A soft blush overcame him, and while not noticeable underneath his beard, Mary felt it.

"Well, let's get that deposit started for you."

Ansel set the paper bag on the counter and unfurled carefully until it took up the width of the banking stall. He reached in, pulled out two large stacks of twenty-dollar bills and slid them towards her. Her eyes set on the stacks, then peered across the hall at her cohort. The man in the suit busied himself with the couple, setting them at ease as only a traveling salesman could before he left town. She cleared her throat and took the stacks across the imaginary line that separated the customer counter from the teller counter. She removed the rubber band with manicured pink nails. It broke quickly, brittle having spent years degrading. She set the first stack of bills in a money counter, then flipped a switch and it whirred into action. Ten seconds. Twenty. Thirty. At forty the obese man's eyebrow perked. Fifty. At sixty his sales pitch faltered slightly.

Mary read the digital readout on the machine and made a notation on a bank deposit slip. As the second stack flowed through, the man cleared his throat and excused himself from the couple. He pressed his plump hands into the armrests to unseat his girth and made his way across the hall to the counter. To Ansel. To Mary.

"Shit," Mary mumbled under her breath.

"Hello sir! I don't believe we met," as he extended his arm at an awkward distance, causing Ansel to consider the ensuing encounter longer than needed.

"Name's Bill, Bill Duerson. Bank manager, Northwest Community Bank."

"Ansel," a pause, "Butler," he responded meekly as he felt the clamminess of Bill's hand penetrate his skin.

"I tell you, Mr. Butler, I make it a point to give my utmost attention to every customer that walks through those doors. How about once you're done here we sit down and discuss the amazing opportunities

Northwest Community has to offer. Loans with great rates. Our new credit card. Did you know that this very summer we're putting in an automated teller machine? I tell you, Mr. Butler, you've done right by being a customer here."

The second stack had finished through the counting machine, and the man's last sentence was abnormally loud in the new quiet. Mary stood silently and observed the two men. It took some time for Ansel to process the information. Not because he didn't understand, but he truly didn't care. He looked through Bill, took in the aroma of cheap cologne and strong peppermint and realized his time to respond was fading into the uncomfortable for the bank manager.

"I don't have much time today. Another time, thank you," said Ansel politely.

"Well that's no problem, Mr. Butler. How's Monday for you?"

"Well," Ansel paused, "I don't know."

"Let's say Monday, the morning good for you?"

"Sure," he said uncertainly.

"Wonderful! Nine, is nine good for you?"

"Yes."

"Well that's just great, I will see you Monday morning at nine," as he extended his hand once more and was reluctantly met. "Monday at nine," Bill uttered as he turned back halfway to the couple. "Your life's gonna get better on Monday, Mr. Butler!"

Ansel returned his attention to Mary as she wrapped one of the stacks with a rubber band and slid it back to him. Atop that a few loose twenties.

"You want to keep this for now," she said in a low voice, leaning in.

"No ma'am, I'd like to deposit all of it today."

"First of all, am I really that old that I'm a ma'am?" she said and chuckled. "Second, no, you'd like to deposit what I have and keep the rest for another day."

"No," he paused, "miss, I'd like to put it all..."

"Mr. Butler," she said sternly with a raised voice, and looked to the man to see if he heard. "What I want you to do is tell me to deposit only this amount," she put her hand on the stack nearest her, "and the rest is yours."

She stood firm, and Ansel set himself to understand the situation. His head cocked left. His lips parted and then closed. He saw sincerity behind her eyes and resigned to this outcome. Besides, the man's interruption had kept him longer from Daniel than he had anticipated or wanted.

"I would like to," Ansel responded, "deposit only the amount you have there under your hand."

"Perfect!" and she went from firm to chipper on a turn.

Deposit slip in his pocket. Brown paper bag folded over cash tucked under his arm. Out the door and he had forgotten the man's name. The appointment slipped into the forgotten.

6

The morning grew. The sun burst down. Keenan sat with a cigarette in a wooden rocking chair rocking against the cracked wood of Ansel's porch, its match nearer the door and separated by a plastic table. The humidity with its sticky residue pressed down on his soft shirt, silk maroon with gold plated buttons exposing his hairy chest. Tucked into tight blue jeans, separated by a brown belt held fast with a similar gold ersatz buckle. He swatted at a honeybee as it circled about him, and it returned to the patchwork bed of arbitrary flowers laid against the home.

The house was set back from the road, as the neighborhood homes were spread out, somewhere between the vastness of farm country and the suburban ideal. There was a sense of privacy and calm not afforded in the city, which made Keenan long to stay and itch to leave.

He rocked, then leaned forward and set the chair still, hearing an engine in the distance. Rubber tires against dirt. For a moment he doubted, yet with a shudder and eyes raised he accepted. A gray sedan flickered through the tree line that paralleled the road. Slowed, then pulled into the driveway and settled behind Keenan's Mercedes. The woman behind the wheel shifted into park, then cut the engine.

"I see this place is still a disaster," Amanda said with a slight smile as she emerged from the car and observed her surroundings.

Keenan dropped the cigarette butt into an empty soda can and walked to the edge of the porch. The sun glinted off her hair, auburn, with bangs and locks that flowed over her shoulders. She had retained the youthful sparkle in her green eyes. A soft pink sundress patterned with pastel flowers lay perfect upon her graceful figure, accessorized with silver bracelets on each wrist.

He stepped off and she stepped forward as pursed lips turned to sappy grins. Near the rusted lawn mower half buried in the grass and dandelions, they embraced.

"It's been too long, Keenan."

"I know."

They released, yet held their hands on each other's shoulders, finding comfort in familiar features and processing the changes.

"Where's Ansel?"

"Don't know, he was supposed to be here."

Keenan walked over to her car. "New car?"

"Yup."

"Chevy?" he asked leaning in the window. Two car seats in the backseat. Folded maps and fast-food wrappers in the front.

"Yup. Citation."

"It's nice."

"Well look at your car, mister big time!" as she walked over to his car. "A Mercedes!"

"Oh it's no big deal."

She ran her hand over the frame. "What was the rule, Keenan?"

"No German cars, no Jap cars."

"I guess it's okay now, isn't it," softly as she peered inside.

"Thought you'd be bringing the girls."

"It's too long of a drive, they'd start to make me crazy halfway here and finish the job by the time we got here."

"I'd like to meet them sometime."

"Anytime, Keenan."

Amanda lifted her hands off the Mercedes and stepped to the porch. She tried the door handle, then cupped her hands over her eyes to see inside. There was a small gap in the drapes, but not enough to discern anything. Keenan lit a cigarette and joined her, choosing the chair nearest the door.

"Where is he? I can't wait to see if it's true."

"So listen, I know we said we'd go today," Keenan started.

"You didn't."

"I didn't do anything; Ansel had already gone."

"One thing! I asked for one thing, that we do this together!"

"I know, I'm sorry."

"Oh, you're sorry!"

"What was I supposed to do! He had already gone! Who knows what he would've done."

"We were supposed to do this together, Keenan."

"I know and I'm sorry."

Amanda sat down on the chair farthest the door.

"We'll go back," Keenan said.

"What for, Keenan? What good is in it?"

Keenan sat down on the empty rocking chair and they sat in silence, looking out past the yard, to the road and beyond at the azure horizon. Both rocking, taking in the space and time. Each delving into memory, then pushing the images down for the next one to creep in. Sometimes allowing the present and future to avail themselves. The phone rang inside, bringing them back.

"I am proud of you, Keenan. Being in New York. Getting out of this place. Making your way."

He listened and decided to forgo a response.

"Just wanted to say so in person, and I know Ansel is too, though he probably hasn't said as much. Also," she added as she rocked softly, "you're a prick for going without me."

The phone rang.

◆ ◆ ◆

The dry dirt kicked up by the tires was visible before the truck. A haze of sunburned earth painted a backdrop beyond the trees, cut with sunlight. Ansel pulled into the driveway fast, bouncing the suspension and settled on the grass to the left of the parked cars. Daniel pushed the door open and shoved it closed with both hands. He ran to the porch, and without an acknowledgement to Keenan jumped on Amanda, his bony knees atop her thighs and skinny arms wrapped around her neck.

"Hi, Aunt Amanda!"

"Hello young man! My, you're getting big!"

Ansel walked slowly from the truck, paper bag in hand. He reached the porch and stood near the door. Amanda stood and Daniel slipped down. She walked with her eyes fixed on Ansel, who again tried to hide any emotion and failed, allowing her embrace.

"You're getting big too," she said as she patted his stomach and laughed. He stepped back, embarrassed.

Keenan cleared his throat and stood.

"Daniel," Ansel started, in response to Keenan's movements, "do you remember your Uncle Keenan?"

The young boy examined the man standing before him.

"It's been a while," said Keenan.

"Since you were about three or four," Ansel said to Daniel.

"I'm sorry, I don't remember," and ashamed, he looked down at the floorboards.

"Hey, hey. Don't worry about it," Keenan reassured, "it's nice to see you again," and he extended his hand, which Daniel shook delicately and quickly.

Ansel swung the screen door open and pressed the key into the lock. The door swung open and the three siblings entered, with Daniel sprinting past them to the television.

"Go play in your room," Ansel said.

"But I want to play Nintendo."

"Not right now."

"But I want to show Aunt Amanda how far I can get."

"Later, go play in your room."

"But..."

"You want me to tell your aunt to take it back?"

"No."

"Then get in your room," Ansel exclaimed with guttural purpose.

Daniel went, stomped his feet then slammed his door shut.

Ansel set the paper grocery bag on the kitchen table near the disorder, then went into his bedroom. Amanda sat down in a chair at the kitchen table. The remaining chairs were piled high with newspapers. Magazines. A dirty plate. Envelopes, opened and otherwise. The table was in similar disarray, save for where Ansel made room earlier. Keenan opened the refrigerator and took a no-name can of soda.

"You want one?"

"Yes, please," Amanda responded as she surveyed her surroundings. "You know we're not leaving here until we clean up this place," she yelled to Ansel in the other room.

Keenan set the sodas on the table and cleared the chairs, relocating all to the counter, already heaped high. Ansel entered and set the toolbox on the table, then pushed the front corners gently with thumbs and forefingers. As before, he clicked open the clasps and lifted.

"Lord almighty," Amanda said slightly above a whisper as she stood.

"Jesus Christ," Keenan added.

"Yeah," said Ansel, feeling he needed to evoke a similar sentiment.

Keenan lit a cigarette without looking. Ansel stared. Amanda bent in and ran her fingers across the metal edges.

An accountant's visor. Rimmed in white. Green translucent to create soft images from the fluorescent flatness that strained eyes. Reading glasses settled. The bridge low and temples secured with a loose leather strap wrapped around the neck. An adding calculator. Operated nimbly with one hand as it clicked figures from memory. A paper curl rolling out, printed numbers and mathematical signs melding under one another out the back of the machine.

Keenan thought of these, having seen these accessories in offices, near trading floors. Beyond the secretaries in endless gray cubicles that extended into nothing, and beyond that, windows and corner offices that lead to cityscapes bending horizons. He found no solace in corner offices, tailored suits—Italian, with fat silk ties. In this moment, no phones rang incessantly, no secretaries with sensual siren voices piercing the repetitive overtures of "Hammel, Morton, Levinson and Associates, how may I direct your call?"

He'd never set in such accommodations, nor had said responsibilities. Yet, as he counted the bills at the kitchen table, jotting figures in pencil on the blank side of a hospital invoice and placing stacks of bills off to the side, he felt the setup he'd seen would've been beneficial.

Ansel's back ached from the night previous. His joints were tight in his fingers. His muscles were warm and pulsed as he bent for fast-food bags, empty cans, bottles, bags of stale chips, and deposited each in a black trash bag. The home was to be spotless by dinner, per Amanda, under threat of a smacking he hadn't felt since childhood. For good measure, and to drive the point home, she would leave and never return if, at bedtime, she didn't feel comfortable resting her head within these walls.

Daniel had his wish, and his aunt not only watched him play Super Mario Bros, but she played and was quite adept at squashing Goombas and kicking Koopa Troopas. He was impressed and studied her hands on the controller in hopes to imitate her success.

"Get out of the way!" Daniel shrieked as Ansel blocked the television as he cleaned.

"Pause it, Daniel!" Amanda added with intensity.

Daniel pressed down hard on the "start" button and the game froze. Ansel turned to them and tried to understand the hatred found in their eyes, staring up at him from the couch. Failing, he resumed his efforts, while remaining cognizant of the television's location. The wires that created tripping hazards from shelf to couch.

The bills were counted, and the original rubber bands discarded, disintegrated with their first touches in ages. Keenan found new ones, shoved among the randomness of a drawer. He snapped the new stacks together and returned each to the toolbox, closing the lid and clicking the clasps shut to define closure. He pushed the metal from him to make space, as far as it would go before setting against the remaining clutter and replaced the emptiness with an ashtray. A match struck, and a few puffs filled the space around the light fixture with gray smoke.

"Well," he started and then hesitated. Setting his cigarette in the ashtray he reached for a paper grocery bag near him on the table. It was the way it was folded, unlike how one would save it after a trip to the store. It was tighter, folded several times and more care was taken here than with any other item in the house.

It was the way the bills were arranged in the toolbox. There was a gap on the left side where easily a stack from the top row could fit. Their father's obsessiveness with organization and symmetry had stuck with Keenan. Cereal boxes were to be set in the pantry by size, the largest farthest left and the panels with the names facing out. He had difficulty driving alone, not due to any phobia or past wreck, but for the imbalance created by an empty passenger seat. Towels matched, as did the sheets on every bed. Tools were organized. Labeled. Some of these quirks had been lost to him as memories faded and the secondhand compulsion receded. Yet, every time he sat down in the driver's seat, he would think about it, then release it as insanity. Every time.

Prior to last night, the last man to touch the inside of this box was his father, and the meticulousness lacking had bothered Keenan from the moment the latch opened. The man he knew would have never left an opening between the stacks and the box wall. He would have filled the gap on the bottom and stacked the remaining on top. To Keenan, this reeked of stupidity, as it would have been easier to fill the bottom row and then the top, thereby exonerating his father. It reeked of carelessness and impulsivity, which he thought implicated someone.

He looked to the living room; Ansel was dusting a bookshelf. Amanda and Daniel busied themselves in the game. With a smooth motion he took the bag and carefully unfurled it, muting the crinkles as best he could. Opened, he reached his hand inside, grasped the rubber-banded cash and slid it out.

"Ansel," Keenan said plainly over the television and the distance between them.

"Ansel," louder when he didn't respond.

Listlessly Ansel rose from a crouch facing the wall and turned to the kitchen, feather duster in hand.

"Come over here."

The tone had prompted Ansel's heart to drop in realization that he had forgotten to tell them. He had forgotten to put the money back in the box. The fact that, hours earlier, he had taken something that was not yet his. He had done this in haste, not to a stranger, but to his kin. He was ashamed and readied himself for the coming outnumbered argument. He walked in front of the television and was reprimanded again. He then stationed himself against the wooden panel ledge dividing the living room from the kitchen for some level of protection, however ineffective.

"What's this?" Keenan asked, holding up the stack of bills.

"I have to," Ansel started, "I had to... well I opened it this morning."

"What did I say?" Keenan's volume rose.

Ansel didn't respond.

"I said we'd all open it together. This morning. Together. And not only did you open it, you took money out."

Amanda had heard the tension grow and turned her attention from the game, though not her eyes.

"I forgot," Ansel let out.

"I forgot. That's the first thing you've said I believe."

Amanda abandoned the game and posted herself between the two men, though set back.

"Stupid son of a bitch," Keenan continued, under his breath but loud enough to hear.

"Watch it, Keenan," chimed Amanda.

"Watch it? He was stealing."

"I wasn't stealin'."

"And he left the evidence right out on the table like an idiot."

"I just wanted to get some in the bank so I could pay the hospital."

"Wait, you went to the bank?"

"Yeah."

"When? This morning?"

"Yeah."

"So there's more you took?"

Ansel was silent in assent.

"How much?" Keenan asked as he stood up fast.

"I don't know."

"You don't know? How does someone not know?"

"I got the receipt in the truck."

"Go get it."

Ansel's grip released from the divider, and he left the interior for the driveway.

"I'm gonna kill him."

"Keenan!" Amanda reprimanded.

"I really am," as he pushed his fists into the table.

"Over what?"

Keenan stood and seethed at an ethereal enemy, his breaths deep through clenched teeth.

"Keenan?"

His breaths deep.

"Keenan?"

Keenan broke his stare with the invisible enemy. He turned to his sister, and she stared, earnest to understand. He wanted to tell her he had nothing left. That there was no penthouse apartment. That he had chosen to drive rather than fly because the Mercedes was all he had left. Because the repo men operate at all hours throughout the boroughs. He wanted her to know his failure. That this was his only chance at redemption. His chance to return to New York City and be what he had told them he has been all this time. He wanted to tell her, but could only laugh to mitigate his embarrassment.

The screen door banged against the wooden frame, then settled awkwardly. Daniel ignored the trespass, as he had anything but the intrusion of space between him and the television. Amanda and Keenan stood near the kitchen table.

Without eye contact, Ansel handed the bank deposit to Keenan. He pushed his glasses up the bridge of his nose and examined the slip.

"Nine thousand, nine hundred and ninety-five dollars," he read, then looked down at the stack upon the paper bag.

"Would've been all of it, but Mary, uh, the teller, she told me not to deposit it all."

"She know you?"

"She... her son knows Daniel."

"What's going on, Keenan?" Amanda asked.

"If he would've deposited more than ten k she'd have to report the transaction to the government."

"And then what?" she followed up.

"Nothing, it's one transaction, there's no pattern. She was just protecting him."

Keenan sat down at the table, lit a cigarette and held it in his hand against his forehead. "I didn't mean to jump on you, Ansel, just a little jumpy being here, that's all."

◆ ◆ ◆

Distant thunder rumbled as dusk pressed. The horizon glowed neon yellow against the horizon, reset, then glowed again. The cicadas stirred. Crickets stretched their wings from slumber, signaling the birds into bedtime song.

Ansel hefted a suitcase from the trunk of Amanda's car and lugged it to the house, and once inside, he set to cleaning as Amanda prepared dinner. On the porch Keenan rocked slowly with a can of Budweiser and waited for the storm.

"Hey," Daniel said, standing over Keenan.

"Jesus Christ!" Keenan jolted, spilling beer on his lap. "Hey, sorry I didn't, uh, I didn't hear you come out." He stood and wiped the beer from his lap.

"Dad says I can't play video games no more tonight. So, are you really my uncle?"

"Yeah," as the word wafted in the humidity, and he sat back down and lit a cigarette. "Yeah, we met when you were real little, when you were just a baby."

"And you live far away?"

"Yeah, New York City."

Daniel sat down on the vacant rocking chair and stared at the neon as it took its time to rumble east.

"So how's school?"

"It's summer."

"Yeah, yeah it is."

"What do you do for fun?"

"Play Nintendo, why'd you wanna kill my dad?"

Keenan held the can mid sip to his lip, then swallowed fully. "Oh I didn't mean that. I was just angry, that's all."

"Then why'd ya say it?"

"You ever get angry and say something you don't mean?"

"I told Tommy Hudson I was gonna kill him."

"See, you were mad and didn't mean it."

"No, I meant it. Still do."

"You want to kill him?"

"Yup," Daniel said and stood up, "I said 'Tommy Hudson! I'm gonna kill you!'" and he pointed to an imaginary boy in the yard.

"Why?"

"Cause he called me 'Skeletor' cause I got real skinny," Daniel explained as he sat back down, "and Michael he didn't say nothin' to stick up for me and I saw him laugh. He didn't think I saw but I did."

"What's 'Skeletor'?"

"He's a bad guy ... he's got a skeleton face."

"He sounds like a pretty bad guy."

"Super bad."

The thunder growled, and the lighting focused. A few drops of rain fell to the tire swing and echoed off the car roofs.

"But it's okay," Daniel continued as if there was no break in his thought, "He-Man always defeats Skeletor."

"Oh yeah?"

"Yeah," Daniel shot from the chair, "whenever he needs to fight Skeletor, he takes out his sword and says 'by the power of Grayskull, I have the power!'" as he thrust his arm above his head. "Then this lighting shoots down and he gets super strong."

"That sounds awesome."

"And he's got a battle cat. Like a real big, like a tiger that's huge."

"Tigers are huge."

"Yeah, but this is so big."

As the rain steadied and the thunder and lightning drew nearer, Daniel felt emboldened by his uncle's engagement. He had been forced inward by Ansel's isolation, and each day compounded the shuttered depression. With each, a deeper sadness manifested in dust. Musty linens and mildew. Decomposed leftovers on stained dishes and ringed glassware.

"What's a 'k'?"

"A 'k'?"

"You said somethin' about 'ten k.'"

"You have ears on you, huh?"

"I hear real good."

Keenan reassured with a quick chuckle. "It means thousand. So I meant ten thousand."

"Dollars?"

"Yeah."

"That's a lot."

"A whole lot."

"Like a million dollars?"

"Well, not that much."

Amanda pressed against the screen door, "Alright boys, dinner time."

7

For the casual traveler, Tony's Truck Stop stocked all the processed necessities for the vacationer. Candy. Potato chips. Soda pop. Coffee. Cigarettes. Packaged sandwiches. Children's toys of pharmacy back aisle quality. They maintained an inventory of CB radios, cab accessories, liquor, and pornography for the trucking men who frequented. The trucking men who'd put miles between the coasts, either pushing east or hauling west. Behind the products and down a narrow white hallway that kept the aroma of cheap disinfectant and dirty mop water close to the sinuses were the restrooms and trucker showers.

Attached to the shop and down a similarly sad hallway was Mae's Restaurant, which, like the truck stop, was open twenty-four hours. Function overmatched form in cracked brown seat pads on booths. On stools. Laminated single-page menus highlighted with steak and eggs, BLTs and soups of the day.

Keenan sat at the counter and added to the potpourri of stale cigarette smoke and bulk coffee heated on high for hours. A trucker busied himself in fried chicken and potato chips several stools down. 'MACK' printed across a greasy, dirty blue cap and his gut rested on his lap. The waitresses were either rotund, having given up, or young and on their way there. He wondered about Rhonda the waitress as she set his change on the counter, then let it pass. There were women who made it out of this speck of nothing along the interstate, then there was Rhonda. Or Heather. Or Pauline. What comfort, he thought, to exist in such simplicity of being. Of basic education, to diner, to mother, to death. Or, similarly, basic education to auto mechanic to death. Or a trucker shoveling deep-fried morsels between his greasy lips in between the miles. He felt an unseen pressure lift as he didn't want, didn't yearn, if only for a few minutes settled on a truck stop stool.

A fluorescent flickered as he passed through the hallway and entered the truck stop. Still philosophical as he inspected the CBs and imagined calling out to his fellow truckers, complaining of unskilled RVers and slow-moving station wagons. Ill-mannered children, throwing the bird from rear-facing seats.

He took a fifth of Jack Daniels from a shelf and walked leisurely down each aisle. Two truckers talked shop by the registers. In the aisle closest to the windows, there were cap guns. Army men. Unbranded dolls. Baseball card packs with stale bubble gum. Matchbox car knockoffs. Two boys ran in front of him as their parents halfheartedly attempted to corral them, and they grabbed and replaced every toy that caught their eyes. While the boys jostled, something caught Keenan's eye as well.

"Pack of Winston's," he said as he put the fifth and the toy on the counter.

"Sure, hon."

Lightning lit the far horizon, but the storm had passed, and the air had cooled. There were only a few cars in the motel parking lot when Keenan pulled his Mercedes over puddles into a spot. His neighbor stood in the entryway to her room, the door ajar. She puffed on a thin cigarette and considered his car in relation to future profits. In her late thirties and lean, owed to a presumed diet of drink, smoke and habit. Thick mascara and eyeliner hid her eyes, and a deep rouge accentuated her lips. Bottled blonde locks set in curlers, and she wore a semi-sheer white robe that wrapped low, exposing her cleavage and a black teddy underneath.

Keenan stepped out of the car with the plastic bag from the truck stop. Opaque, the woman slipped her eyes downward to inspect the contents as he arrived in front of his door.

"Looks like you got a fun night planned, hon," as she motioned with her eyes to the bag, a slight Southern twang in her voice.

"Yeah, I guess," while fumbling in his pocket for his room key.

"I could make it more fun, if you know what I mean." She subtly lifted her robe a few inches.

He looked her over once more and imagined himself lifting her robe and teddy, exposing her panties. "Thank you kindly," and cleared his throat, "I'm all set."

"Alright, hon. If you change your mind, all you gotta do is knock."

A breeze brushed over the walkway that lined the building and he took in her perfume. Floral that evoked the feminine. Musk that lowered inhibitions in the moment and altered the power structure between the sexes. He took it all in, then clumsily slid the key into the lock and pushed his way in, locking the deadbolt behind him.

Absent were the plush lounge chairs on rooftop bars nestled between high-rises. Absent was the stale cigar smoke on the fiftieth floor. Absent three-piece suits and crystal rocks glasses. Keenan took a Styrofoam cup from the dresser set near the plastic coffee maker. He sat down at the table, unsealed the Jack and poured liberally. The first sip was harsh, and he swallowed hard. Once it steadied and warmed him, he took another. A third and he lit a cigarette.

The interstate rushed as he pulled open the window. The rain had cleansed. Washed away the dust of pulsing August heat and the dry bristling of ripe corn fields swaying in humid breezes. It brought about virgin memories in the grown, and new understandings in the pubescent minds loitering in cars idling in abandoned parking lots. Drink, coupled with the cash he had in his wallet, of which he dutifully noted in the hospital invoice ledger, had reinvigorated his libido. Release pressed on his mind, the convenience of which being only steps away. He thought of her naked body against his. Her perfumed skin perfuming his. The rush of illegality and the memory of cocaine-fueled lust perpetrated in penthouse apartments owned by men of low morality and particular lifestyle standards. He cursed the obligatory regret that would creep in the waning moments of lucidity before sleep and elevated the sweet feminine aroma that calms a man into dream.

He took charge of the remaining whiskey in the cup, and as his resolve fortified, he saw a man appear through the window. A shadow in the darkness of the frontage road, beyond which the truck stop stood. Under the parking lot lights, though dim, he saw he was young, tall, svelte and clad in a mustard yellow tank top with contoured muscles exposed. His cheeks were taught, shadowed by a brown cowboy hat. Tight blue jeans tucked into cowboy boots. Keenan watched his approach and first defended his own wrinkles, gut and graying hair with the absurdity of the man's ensemble. Upon more honest consideration, no silk shirt he owned could compensate. As with most drunken thought, the logic appeared last: there were no differences between the two men in any transaction conducted in room number eight at the Keyes Motel.

The cowboy trucker knocked, and within seconds, the door opened.

"Well hello there, handsome," she said, and Keenan heard through the open window, "C'mon in!"

Keenan opened the bottle and refilled the cup. He could only wait to satiate his urges, but his neighbor's window was open, and he could hear every grunt, every moan. Every apology a young man makes the first time in the company of an older woman as he thinks each movement is examined and graded. Every reassurance whispered in his ear as he glistened with effort. Every pause he made to alleviate release. In its duration, Keenan closed his motel window.

His lust had faded, and he resigned himself to weariness and half-drunken slumber. He closed his eyes and a night from his teenage years came back to him. At first, he tried to shake the memory, yet it kept coming back...

Flicker, flicker, as a bonfire crackled in a clearing behind the barn. It warmed the teenage boys and girls as spring had warmed the days but had yet to breach the nights. Four boys lined a pickup bed, puffing and drinking. High school seniors. Hippies, as much as they could be, geographically isolated in the rural expanse, and they plotted at this moment to change their circumstances. A boy playing Dylan's "Don't Think Twice, It's All Right" on a beat-up acoustic guitar. Then, "Mr. Tambourine Man," then, another Dylan song.

"My God man," Keenan reprimanded under his breath as he dwelled in the shadows of the bonfire, "learn someone else's fucking music."

Ansel sat on an upturned log, clean shaven and thick with muscle. His girlfriend pressed against him and wore his varsity sweater, dark green with a prominent white "B" sewn on one side. His selected service was selected, set to report for his armed forces physical examination in a week. Amanda sat on a folding chair, her boyfriend maintaining appropriate distance in the presence of her two brothers. Partly out of fear, as Ansel was captain on the wrestling team, and partly out of respect for the future soldier.

Keenan's legs dangled from the edge of a pickup bed opposite the hippies, a slow sway with a Miller can and a Lucky Strike. Every so often, he'd have the courage to look to his left. He had kept the crush secret, as memory instructed in him rejection in pursuit of the female form.

Black hair in perfect curls ran down past her shoulder blades, framed her emerald eyes and commanding, yet inviting features. A button-down flannel shirt, faded yellow with a subtle brown crosshatch. Light blue jeans, frayed and split at the knees, exposing her soft, pale skin in the fire light. A bottle of Boone's strawberry wine in one hand and a menthol cigarette in the other.

He stole another glance, but this time she caught him, and his stomach dropped as she smiled coyly and closed her eyes in her returned focus to the guitarist. Several verses. A chorus. A coda.

"Hey, Tommy!" a hippie yelled, "You play any more Dylan I'm gonna break that gee-tar!"

Keenan flicked his cigarette near the flames, hopped off the steel bed, and ambled beyond the bonfire. He unzipped his blue jeans with beer bottle in hand, swayed slightly as set his legs apart, steadied, and emptied his bladder against the barn wall. In relief, he zipped and buttoned, pulled his belt tight, and turned back to the teenage cluster. The guitarist took several swigs from a bottle of Coors and readied the guitar and set his pick. A satisfying, communal sigh bellowed as he saw a red door and wanted to paint it black.

Keenan mused pursuing his teenage lust. The fire danced shadows against her features and accentuated the softness assumed between her legs. Illuminated the line that separated her breasts exposed with buttons undone. Yet the musings were superseded by the denials that overrode his desire. Denial amid the chaotic background of school hallways. Around young women congregating in cafes. On school buses.

He grabbed a fresh bottle and cracked it open with a bottle opener. He pulled the barn door open quickly and slipped into the dark interior, now set with harsh shadows from the fire. He made his way to the loft ladder from memory, and even in drunkenness climbed steadily. Stepped upon strewn hay then pulled a bale forward and reached among dog-eared novels, yellowed comic books. A Bible. Candy bar wrappers. Blankets. His arm stretched past empty soda cans and grasped a lantern by its handle, setting it on the floor. He primed the kerosene pump, then took a matchbook from his jacket pocket. A deep breath as he struck the sulfur head against the coarse surface, ready to strike out any errant spark in the hay or leap from the height. As he had done many nights in hiding. As had Amanda.

The flame held in place, and he slid the match into the lantern and it whooshed, bathing the loft in gas-fueled light. He adjusted the flow and his surroundings dimmed into a warm aura.

His crush had watched his escape, had seen him disappear from the interior shadows and spied the lantern flash. She hopped from the truck bed, walked around the fire, and slid between the barn doors. Using the lantern light as a guide, she climbed the ladder to the loft, the Boone's bottle knocked against the wood rungs.

His heart jumped as she appeared at the top rung. He was trapped, and with that decision made for him, he took a swig of beer and accepted the situation. She sat across from him, separated by the lantern. Both on makeshift seats of hay bales, and he was silent and flipped a bottle cap he found in his pocket between his fingers. She took stock of the lantern, then the hay surroundings, then returned to him.

"Fuck Dylan," Jennifer said as she broke the silence, then followed up with a swig of wine. Keenan smiled, then hid the emotion.

"Blowin' in the wind, my ass," he said, reassured by the safety of the loft.

"Right?!" as she pulled a menthol from her shirt pocket. He eyed the subtle pressure on her breast.

"Got a match?"

He stood up, walked to her, crouched down and with rare smoothness in teenage awkwardness sparked the match head. The flame settled, he held it to her cigarette then shook it out and returned to his spot on the floor.

"So you think you'll go? Like your brother?"

"How'd you know he's going?"

"I have three older brothers. I know."

"Well he's gotta go through basic, and that takes a while. War'll probably be over by the time I gotta go."

"And if it's not?"

"I'll say I got something wrong with me. Bone spurs or something."

The guitarist had taken a break, and the mumbles of conversation creeped into the loft. The sound of kerosene through the lantern covered any inadvertent silence down below.

"It's cold up here."

"You get used to it," he said quickly, then realized she sought a solution. He stood and reached into the shadowy corner and pulled out a blanket. He shook it out, then walked around the lantern to her seat of hay and he draped the maroon and yellow wool over her shoulders. He stepped back, and she grabbed his hand, drawing him close. He took a swig of beer as he sat. Away from the smoke and cinder he caught her perfume. Floral. Musk. Her arm wrapped around him to hand off the blanket fringe, which he took to envelop them both. In the loft, he had banished unrequited desire. Evicted false expectations and the authenticity of daydreams realized. He had worked hard to create in it a safe space for him and Amanda. While he thought Jennifer's cues warranted an action, he had misread girls before to great embarrassment and depression. What then, if this place became tainted, he thought. Fouled with renewed rejection?

"Keenan?" she asked in the stillness, giving him opportunity to look at her. "What do you want outta life?"

He peered at the floor, hoping an answer would carve into the wood. "I don't know."

"Me either."

She pressed into him and he put her arm around her. Under the blanket against the soft cotton of her shirt, his thumb brushed against her skin hidden under curls. She took a puff and pressed the butt into the floor as she cleansed her palette with cheap strawberry wine and turned to him. The thought of her pursuing him made him feel a loss of accomplishment, but that faded quickly with a cocked neck and closed eyes. In each pursuit previous his lips had met with air, and he braced himself for that inevitability. And under kerosene light, he kissed his first. Her lips were moist with strawberry wine and tasted of menthol. Her tongue darted to meet his. His hand ran up her button-down flannel shirt without even a tinge of pullback. He was relaxed in reciprocation, in his saving the sanctity of this place. The only nerves that remained were in her willingness to continue, and to what extent.

8

The morning heat had dried all residual moisture as Ansel guided a green push mower over the grass blades and weeds and the engine belched exhaust. He pushed the tire swing to one side and navigated the elder tree in a tank top that exposed his hairy shoulders. Below, paint-splattered jeans and the work boots.

Keenan stepped out of the Mercedes in a deep brown cotton blend shirt tucked into khakis. About the wheel wells, caked in dirt, rough earth splattered the beige paint. He took note of Ansel's activity, then opened the trunk. He took out a heavy paper grocery bag and tucked a wiffle ball set under his armpit to free a hand and close the trunk. With a light step, he hopped to the porch and pulled the screen door open.

It clunked shut, then bounced to stillness. He walked through the living room, noticed the cleanliness of it all and the smell of lemon and the television's absence. He set the bag and the toy down on the counter near the stove.

"I got breakfast!" he bellowed—with no response—then took a mug from a cabinet and poured a cup of coffee from the glass carafe. It sizzled as he set it on the warmer. At the table, he noticed a chair was missing, then lit a Winston and sipped. He heard commotion down the narrow hallway that led to the bathroom. The television in Daniel's room. The mower buzzed alongside the house.

"Good morning, Keenan," Amanda said, as she adjusted an earring. She was dressed proper in the early hour: a purple dress accentuated with a gold necklace bearing a simple cross.

"You look nice for a Sunday."

"I look nice *because* it's Sunday."

"Church?"

"Yeah, church. And you're coming with." She set to unpacking the grocery bag. A carton of eggs. Bacon. A loaf of white bread. An orange juice carton. Bologna. American cheese.

"Shit."

"And that's why. Uncouth language and sinful living … it can't hurt to pray, and Lord knows it's been a while for you."

"We don't have time for that. We have plenty to do here."

"There's always time for church."

"Is Ansel going?"

"No, he has to look after Daniel."

"Where's the toolbox?" Keenan asked as he looked at the table.

"I hid it. Didn't seem right to keep it out in the open."

"What about the ledger?"

"You mean your scribbles?"

"Yeah."

"In the box."

Keenan leaned against the counter. His aim was to secure his portion and leave, yet he had promised to stay a little longer.

"Look what I got, it's for Daniel," he said as he took the wiffle bat in his hand.

"That's a nice gesture."

"Figured we could hit some balls this morning. He still sleeping?"

"He's not well this morning, best to let him rest."

"No?"

"Sometimes the drugs take their toll. Some days worse than others."

He paused, then went to Daniel's room.

"Daniel?" with a soft knock and no reply. He turned the knob and pressed the door. Through the gap Daniel was under a blanket up to his neck, knees pulled tight against his stomach. He faced the television that Ansel had moved into the room and placed on a chair, the bunny ear antenna atop the set. Keenan walked in and smelled the lemon cleanser, though it was overwhelmed by the fresh vomit in a plastic bucket, set close enough for Daniel to roll to in necessity.

"Hey bud," as he sat softly on the end of the bed, "it's your Uncle Keenan." He held the wiffle set in his lap. "How you feelin'?"

"Sunday morning cartoons are crap," he said without moving.

Keenan had no frame of reference to respond. Were they crap in general? Crap compared to other cartoons, aired at a different time? "Mind if I open the window?"

Daniel didn't respond. Keenan took that as consent and opened the window, and a breeze blew in with the aroma of freshly cut grass. He returned to the bed; this time closer. "Look what I got you."

He cocked his neck with pupils elevated. "A baseball bat?"

"It's wiffle bat. And ball. So you can play ball in the front yard without worrying about breaking a window."

Daniel was uninterested and set his eyes on the television.

"You know, I used to play baseball."

"On a team?"

"Yup. Got as far as the minor leagues."

He waited for Daniel's reaction, which didn't come.

"I played shortstop. For the Toledo Mud Hens."

"What's a 'Mud Hen'?"

"It's a baseball team in the minor leagues."

"No, I mean what's a 'Mud Hen'?"

Keenan went silent for a moment, "Hell, I don't know. Guess it's some kind of bird."

"What does it look like?"

"I don't know."

"You should find out."

"Okay, I will."

"I mean now."

"What?"

"I don't want no company right now."

Keenan stood from the bed and looked the boy over. Took in the blanket cocoon. He set the wiffle bat near him and started out the door.

"You can take that," Daniel said from under the blanket. Keenan stood in silence. "I ain't got no friends to play it with." And with that, Keenan looked down at his shoes, rummaged his mind for a response to no avail, then took the bat and closed the door quietly.

He grabbed his coffee mug from the table and replaced it with the bat, then went to the porch. Ansel saw him and cut the mower.

"Hey, Ansel."

"Hot day," as he wiped the sweat from his forehead with a blue bandana.

"Hot day indeed. Your boy alright?"

"Doctors think they got it beat, just gotta get through this round of chemo."

"Good, good," Keenan said between sips. "I have to go to church with Amanda, and when I get back we'll divide it up."

Ansel looked down at the mower, then back at Keenan.

"You're not gonna go running off with the money, are ya?" Keenan asked with a smile.

Ansel didn't react, and instead pulled the cord to start the mower. It sputtered for a few seconds then hummed. He looked to the porch and nodded to his brother, who in turn, raised his coffee mug slightly in acknowledgement. Ansel guided the green push mower over the grass blades and weeds.

◆ ◆ ◆

'He is before all things, and by Him, all things hold together,' read the sign in black block letters set near the entrance. The church itself was a small L-shaped brick building, with a faded burgundy roof that came to a point in the center and ran the length of the chapel. The steeple was of simple design and matched the hue of the roof. Weeds sprouted through the cracks in the paved parking lot, with station wagons, pickup trucks, and sedans with rust around their wheel wells.

It was their first time in the chapel, yet Amanda meandered through families and greetings as though she'd been there for years. She spoke to the intricacies of baking cupcakes with a portly woman, anchored by her portly husband in a fat tie that didn't quite make it to his beltline. She spoke to Mary Baker from the bank about visiting family and, having introduced herself as Amanda Johnson, née Butler omitted, Mary did not make the connection between Ansel and Amanda.

Keenan had found the pew nearest the back and planted himself there. He resigned himself to prayer, singing, and a sermon that he would find fault with and that was destined to go on forever. He thumbed through a Bible, secure that he had gone this long not believing and reading a verse or two would not change anything.

Having satisfied her social itch, Amanda joined her brother in the pew. Normally she would have dragged her children, or in this instance, her brother, straight up the aisle to the first pew. Yet they were guests here, and she would have felt guilty had they taken another family's usual seats.

"Sing to the Lord, all the earth!" the pastor started from the pulpit. "Tell of his salvation from day to day. Declare his glory among the nations, his marvelous works among all the peoples! For great is the Lord, and greatly to be praised, and he is to be held in awe above all gods."

"Amen," called the congregation.

"And a good morning to you all," the pastor continued, "well, I think our prayers were answered 'cause we had some rain yesterday and there's more to come they say. I was talking to Glenn out in the hallway outside the men's room and boy, he agreed, did we need it. It is great to see you all here this morning. Brother Leyland will lead our singing this morning, and if you take a look at your program, Mike Jones will do the prayer, Dave Baldwin, the communion."

Keenan drifted off almost immediately. The sound of a preacher's voice, coupled with the hard, cold wood made him simultaneously antsy and exhausted in the pew. He reached to tug on a necktie that wasn't there. His legs itched as he imagined the wool slacks he wore as a child. He waited for a pinch on his arm as his eyelids grew heavy. The women's choir, at once loud and mixed with perfect-key soprano and contralto imperfections, roused him. He watched and trained his ear on the singers who could harmonize and attempted to tune out those of less ability.

Amanda knew the words and sang with the congregation. She knew when to stand. When to say "amen." When to smile, when to laugh, and when to be somber.

"The ax is already at the root of the trees," an elderly clergyman bellowed. He had been saving his vocal energy through the week for this moment, "and every tree that does not produce good fruit will be cut down and thrown into the fire. I baptize you with water for repentance. But after me comes one who is more powerful than I, whose sandals I am not worthy to carry. He will baptize you with the Holy Spirit and fire. His winnowing fork is in his hand, and he will clear his threshing floor, gathering his wheat into the barn and burning up the chaff with unquenchable fire. The Book of Matthew."

The preacher stood and joined the clergyman at the pulpit, taking his hand in his and setting the other on his shoulder. He took his place and commenced a sermon on forgiveness. However hard, one must forgive, he said, and even in the deepest transgression—forgive. "For if you forgive other people when they sin against you, your heavenly Father will also forgive you. But if you do not forgive others their sins, your Father will not forgive your sins." Through story, he had awoken Keenan, and in scripture, he had lost him. He placed his head in his hands and smelled the stale smoke on his fingertips, his boredom now lurched along with nicotine withdrawals.

◆ ◆ ◆

Amanda had stayed rapt through the entire service. Her thoughts connected the words and songs to her own family. She tied parables to action items at home for herself and at school for her children. Sought meaning in the sibling reunion and comfort for Daniel. Looked for spiritual advice for their present situation, in possession of something seemingly tainted but that could do so much good.

As the service ended, Keenan was the first to stand, the first to exit to the lobby, and the first to push open the exterior door leading to the parking lot. He lit a cigarette under an awning under sunshine as the western sky darkened with deep gray clouds that bordered on night. Amanda made a social egress and exchanged pleasantries, nothings and quick recaps of her "loving husband and two beautiful children." He *was* loving, and they *were* beautiful. Yet, after expressing it with that exact wording in that exact smile exposing her bright white teeth on so many occasions, she felt like an actor reciting lines. It was partially her fault, which she accepted as a social butterfly.

The impending storm cooled the air, and the Mercedes cruised with the windows rolled down and baseball on the radio. Baseball, she thought, was boring to watch. Baseball was even more boring on television. Baseball, she screamed in her head, was intolerable on the radio.

But it wasn't her car, and she felt no desire to interrupt whatever serenity this was. It had been five years since she had last seen Keenan, but she knew he was in no mood to converse. The radio announcer called a strike and imparted statistics pertaining to left-handed batters in this type of heat against the pitcher. In temperate climates. In cold Aprils. His cohort dryly responded with hot dog etiquette. A foul ball, and on to the proper toppings, ballpark versus backyard barbecue. Ball two. Ketchup? Chicago?

It was insufferable, and she pulled her mind from it and saw herself as a young girl. She imagined her childhood legs dangling over the tool bench inside the shed next to the barn. Loose blue overalls and bare feet that swayed. She held her doll over the ledge, told her to be careful, for she could fall and then pulled her close, 'saving' her from certain death. Her father stood next to her and wiped a crescent wrench with a dirty rag, then held it up to inspect each metal turn.

"What's this one?" her father asked, holding the tool aloft.

She turned from her doll. His hands were thick, and his forearms pressed against his flannel shirt, rolled up just below his elbows.

"A wrench," she answered.

"I know, but what kinda wrench?"

"I don't remember," she finally responded, after a pause.

"Crescent wrench."

He set the wrench in its proper place within the toolbox, then picked up a screwdriver and ran the rag along the shaft.

"And this one?"

"Screwdriver! A flathead one."

He smiled and set it in the box.

"And this one?"

"Um."

"See it's different from a flathead," and he pressed his index finger against the pointed tip.

"I don't remember."

"A Philip's head screwdriver."

"Girls don't getta do shop," he said as he cleaned a socket wrench, "no girl of mine ain't gonna know how to fix stuff."

And at once, she was twelve. It was near dusk as she walked alongside the creek that ran the length of the farm acreage and disappeared into the tree line beyond the fields. Along the muddy earth that dove steeply into the water where she first allowed herself to think about boys. And in the gurgling water, a red tractor lay inverted and atop a box wagon, filled with gray cinder blocks upright in the water. In between, her father lay pinned. Unconscious as blood seeped down and dyed the cinder blocks before comingling in the water and washing away in the slow current. The doctors and nurses x-rayed his mangled back. They reset his leg and stitched his forehead as he explained that he had been shoring up the creek bank with cinder blocks. The heavy rains had accelerated the erosion in several places, that was why it was almost dusk and he was still working. As he reversed the tractor in the fading light, the box wagon's tires slipped and the weight of the blocks pulled the tractor down the steep embankment. The back of the wagon hit hard, and the front end of the tractor lifted and flipped.

As he lay in the hospital bed, Amanda heard the story repeated. Sometimes, he had the tractor in reverse gear. Other times, neutral. Some days, he worried about the farm. Some days, he quizzed her by holding up imaginary tools. Other days, he could not comprehend what she was doing in the Ardennes but put the thought aside as he lectured Keenan and Ansel on German positions.

And at once, she was fourteen. The farm had simply become a house. Her father's thick forearms were replaced by reedy appendages. His breath was rich with whiskey to mask the pain coursing along his vertebrae. She would run to the tool shed and study each tool in the box. She'd take them out one by one and then replace them to the sound of screaming and howling and sobbing.

And at once, she was eighteen and her father's anger had retreated. His strength had rebounded, and he found himself in sales, traveling from town to town. And after some time, the heated discussions of money at the kitchen table ceased.

And in the evening before he was set to take her to college, she walked the length of the creek and listened to the babbling and prayed in silence where she had found him. She listened to the cicadas and katydids and wondered what music the night would bring outside the dormitory.

She opened the tool shed door and pulled the dangling string attached to the light bulb. The rakes and hoes and brooms were aligned and hung from hooks against a pegged wall. The bench itself was empty, the black toolbox gone.

In the morning, her mother sobbed against her shoulder and half-heartedly begged her to stay, though she knew this must happen. And as her father drove her down interstates and through small towns, she hoped that he would reveal the toolbox as a present. That he had hid it away in the trunk of the car. That she had earned it by learning each tool and its function and that he couldn't see her without it. Yet he left her in her dormitory room with only the awkward speech that only a father can give so he can save face and hold back tears. He probably knows there are custodians here, she thought. She'll have it soon enough.

"I thought that was a lovely church. Lovely service," Amanda said from the passenger seat, over the game and the road noise.

Keenan smoked and concentrated on the road.

"What'd you think?"

"I didn't pay attention."

"Oh c'mon. Tell me one thing you learned."

"Really? You're gonna act like ma? 'Tell me one thing you learned at church today?'"

"You loved it," she goaded.

"Every fucking Sunday."

"Hey. Watch that *New York* language."

He shot her a glance, as curse words were not locked geographically.

"So," she prodded, "one thing you learned and one thing you prayed for."

"You really want to do this?"

"I do," as she turned off the radio.

"Well, I learned that preacher is full of... full of it."

"I thought he was great."

"There are some things you just can't forgive."

"But you have to, Keenan, even if it's something terrible."

"And if I don't?"

"Then God won't forgive you."

"So if I don't forgive someone, then God won't forgive me? For what? Not forgiving them? That doesn't make sense."

"I think he was saying that if someone does something to you, you have to forgive them, that way God can forgive you for all the bad things you've done."

"And what if God does something to you?"

"God doesn't sin."

"Well he sure didn't do Daniel no favors."

"That's not fair."

"Didn't do Ansel any favors either."

"That's not fair, Keenan."

"What? Life?"

"You can't blame God for our trials," she said agitated with a raised voice, "He doesn't give us nothing we can't handle."

Keenan saw her agitation and saw no sense in continuing.

"God put us all here together," she continued, "after so many years we are here, that's God's doing. You know, only you, Keenan, could turn so quick on such an uplifting and spiritual church service."

With several miles remaining, he had ample opportunities to apologize and defuse the tension but instead held fast with self-righteousness.

"What'd you pray for?" he asked.

"Daniel. I prayed for Daniel."

"Me too," he said as they pulled into the driveway. Although in truth, he also prayed that his greed and lust would be satiated in short order. She didn't need to know. Nobody needed to hear that stated aloud.

The storm had traveled fast. The edge of the disturbance dumped rain, yet the violence wouldn't arrive for another twenty minutes or so.

Daniel remained in bed, drifting in and out of sleep. With the television tied up, Ansel had taken to studying the piles of cash at the kitchen table. He looked over the ledger and its simple arithmetic. He sipped burnt coffee and smoked a cigarette. He picked up the wiffle bat, set it on his shoulders as if he was at the plate and swung slowly, then set it back down.

Keenan and Amanda walked in. She checked in on Daniel then placed her hands lovingly on Ansel's shoulders from behind. He went straight for the fridge and a beer.

"Ready to do this?" said Keenan plopping down in a chair.

"Daniel didn't want this?" Ansel asked, motioning to the bat.

"Nope, said he doesn't have any friends."

"I'll talk to him. Don't take nothing he says too seriously when he's hurting bad."

"Oh it's alright."

"Anyone'd get mean in pain," Ansel said, defending Daniel.

"So, the cash, I say we just..."

"We prayed good for him this morning," interrupted Amanda, "didn't we Keenan?"

"We did."

"And I got to thinking, sitting in that nice church, have you been Ansel?"

"No. I mean not since, not in a few years."

"I told the pastor you'd go if you want, and he said if you do, you and Daniel are always welcome."

"I ain't gonna go."

"I know," as she squeezed his shoulders in understanding.

"Guys," Keenan implored, "let's focus here."

"Alright, Keenan," as she released and sat down, "what are your thoughts on this treasure before us?"

"It's simple, there's three of us, we each get a third."

"It's not that easy, Keenan," she responded, "there might be three of us, but we are *not* even."

"Maybe so, but how's that fair?"

"You're serious?"

"A third is fine," Ansel said.

"No, it's not."

"See, Ansel agrees," said Keenan.

"I saw your hospital bills," as she looked at Ansel, "a third is not fine. And you," turning her attention to Keenan, "what, you don't have enough with your Mercedes and fancy city apartment and your silk shirts? You need more? Huh?"

"Well what do you suggest if we ain't dividing it equally?"

"I suggest a thousand for me, a thousand for you, and the rest for Daniel."

"Really? You couldn't use more?" Keenan asked his sister.

"Of course I could, but what's right is right."

"This is all of ours."

"Ours to decide the right way to do this. Did church do nothing for you this morning?"

"I just think thirds is fair."

"You don't need it, Keenan, Daniel does."

Again, Keenan wanted to stand up and scream 'Yes, I do!' He wanted to admit to being hustled by Wall Street boys who competed for the title of worst human being ever. He needed the money to compete. The anger swelled. Swelled. Crested. Crashed and rolled softly against the beach, steadied into the reality of Daniel's situation. Of Ansel's.

"Fine, a thousand for me an you, the rest for Daniel, by way of Ansel."

"Well," she started, "I'm glad to see you've come to your senses. Then it's settled."

"It ain't settled," growled Ansel, and his siblings quieted immediately.

"You're right, Amanda, a third of this won't cover what I owe at the hospital. But this is sufferin' money, and you two suffered good."

They knew there were two men hidden under Ansel's beard, in addition to regular, everyday Ansel. Keenan and Amanda had created this hypothesis years ago, about the time it started to grow in, after his tour in Vietnam. 'Wise Ansel' was quiet, his words crafted and true, akin to an Indian Chief. There was no hesitation in his voice, and the truth rose supreme in any conversation. 'Hillbilly Ansel' was quiet as well and without hesitation, but the words pinballed incoherently as if neurons were misfiring, yet he remained unaware. Both 'wise' and 'hillbilly' started off the same, but it was where they ended up that classified each encounter. The younger siblings at once cued on the phrase "Sufferin' money," and waited on an Ansel to show himself.

"Way I see it," Ansel started, "we all grew up together, so this treasure is ours to share. I ain't never asked nothing from you two, and you know it. Amanda, you're right about the bills, I need to get square with the hospital. Need another thousand to bribe the foreman over at the Ford plant in Mayville to get me on the line. If that don't work, gotta go get my mechanic's certification. Daniel wants a VCR so he can record his cartoons, and I'm inclined to oblige. That leaves plenty for you and Allan and the girls. Plenty for you, Keenan, for whatever the hell you do with money ... maybe get you a shirt that don't make you look like a pretty boy an' get an American car."

The younger siblings said nothing in response. 'Wise Ansel' had spoken, and thus resolved the disagreement. Keenan stood from the table and got three cans of Budweiser from the refrigerator and brought them to the table. He opened each and handed one to Amanda, one to Ansel. They clinked dull aluminum in understanding then each took a long sip.

9

It had been twenty minutes, or an hour, since Ansel had washed his face and brushed his teeth. Shirtless, he stood at the sink in front of the mirror. He pulled down his thick beard. Stared at his eyes as they stared back. The wrinkles that had formed. Dark chest hairs being invaded by gray. His gut, as it had grown. In the late hour, he breathed slowly with fastened lips.

It had been twenty minutes, or an hour, when the sound of the television broke his posture and he left the bathroom. He walked past his bedroom, where Amanda slept, down the narrow hallway and pushed Daniel's bedroom door open. He sat down on the bed, next to the young child who held a Nintendo controller and sat with legs crossed facing the screen.

"You hungry?" Ansel asked softly while watching the television.

"Nah."

"Thirsty?"

"Nah."

"Feelin' better?"

"Yeah."

Ansel got up and went to the kitchen. He took a glass from the cabinet and filled it with tap water from the sink.

"Here," as he handed the glass to Daniel and sat back down, "drink so you don't get dehydrated."

Daniel paused the game and took the glass from his father. He took a small sip to test his gag reflex, then gulped steadily until it was empty. Ansel took the glass and set it on the dresser. There, unopened, the wiffle bat and ball rested, and he picked it up.

"You like the present your uncle got you?" as he sat down again.

"I guess," as he focused on the video game.

"I think it's really nice."

Daniel ignored him.

"You know," Ansel said, "your uncle played baseball. Not the Majors but close."

He continued with his game.

"You need to apologize to your uncle."

"I don't even know him."

"Doesn't matter."

"I don't like him."

"Doesn't matter."

"I won't mean it."

"Doesn't matter," Ansel said with the same monotone as previous, "I ain't askin' you to like him right away. Just be nice."

"I don't wanna."

Ansel sighed, then set his hand on the back of Daniel's neck, who felt the warmth. "I know you don't wanna, but it's important to be a big kid sometimes. And sayin' you're sorry is a very big kid thing for you to do. Besides, only big kids get to play Nintendo."

◆ ◆ ◆

Keenan leaned against the motel room door and faced the parking lot as he smoked a cigarette and sipped on a Budweiser can. The night was warm, crickets conversed when the interstate was sparse, a trucker grunted exertion, and his neighbor moaned just enough to keep him feeling alpha. A phone rang in one of the rooms. A station wagon drove past Keenan and pulled into a parking spot. A weary father took his child from the backseat and put her to his shoulders in slumber. A mother took note of the carnal activities and Keenan at the door, but not the crickets. She opened the door to their room and turned on the lights. He followed with the child then returned to gather suitcases and travel bags. The door shut, and the lock clicked. The trucker reached his crescendo and breathed heavily. After climax, he must have realized shame and risk, for he dressed quickly and exited with a brisk pace across the parking lot to his rig.

Keenan stayed against the door. He had sat all morning in church. He had sat all afternoon at Ansel's. He settled into the space and the air and the dim lights and the stars. In all of this was his childhood and his teenage years and the aroma of nothing that kept pulling on him. There was no feeling in the cacophony of car horns echoing against skyscrapers through boroughs emanating pastrami on rye or fried tortillas. He took another Winston from the crumpled pack on the windowsill. Struck another match. Took another drink.

"Well hey there stranger," said his neighbor, startling him. She wore the same semi-sheer white robe and black teddy from the night before, though her hair was done, and her makeup faded some from the evening's work.

"Well hey to you." Keenan responded more confidently than their first sober encounter.

"You got one of those for me?"

"Yeah, sure."

She walked barefoot to his door as he knocked a cigarette from the soft pack and handed it to her. She placed it between her maroon lips. He flicked a match against the matchbook, it flickered, and he cupped the small flame with his hand as she leaned in. He took in her perfume as she pulled in smoke, but in this proximity, he could smell her prior company as well.

"What's your name, stranger?" she asked.

"Keenan," as he shook the match dead, "and yours?"

"Candy."

"That's a pretty name."

"Hope so, I picked it out," Candy said with a smile. "I like your style, Keenan. Nice shirts and pants and all. Definitely different than what I'm used to."

"Thanks."

"Like your car too."

"It's a nice car."

Keenan finished his beer with the last gulps.

"Say, um," he started, "you want to come in?"

"Oh, sorry hon, I only do business in my room."

"Oh, no. I meant, for a drink."

"We can drink right here. Can't be missin' out on any business that come by."

"Sure. Sure."

"Well I'm gonna get another beer, you want one?"

"Don't drink beer, hon."

"Whiskey?"

"Sounds good."

Keenan opened the door, but didn't go in. "You sure you don't wanna come in? Just to talk?"

"Jus' to talk, huh? No offense, but I don't trust pretty boys who jus' want to talk."

He let it go, went into his room and poured two whiskeys in Styrofoam cups. He walked back through the open door but only caught the back of her white robe trailing as she closed her motel room door shut.

He poured the contents of one cup into the other, then stacked the empty under and took a sip, then walked to the motel office. The motel manager was dressed in a brown suit, as the hour was more reasonable than their last encounter. It hung awkwardly from his slender frame. His gray tie with maroon stripes hung loosely from a white collared shirt.

"Ah, Mr. Butler. Will you be extending your stay with us, or are you checking out in the morning?"

"Actually, yeah. Yeah, another night, please."

"Very good."

"Can I get change for a dollar?"

"Of course," as he pulled four quarters from the till and took the bill.

"Thank you ... where's the pay phone?"

"Right outside to your right sir."

"Thank you."

"Are you paying for the extra night now, sir?"

"Ugh, my wallet is in my room."

"Very good, sir. By 9 AM then."

Keenan nodded, then left the office and took the phone receiver to his ear, depositing two quarters in the slot. He looked up and away in thought as the dial tone hummed. With the numbers recalled, he dialed.

"Hey, Jimmy? Yeah it's Keenan. Keenan Butler. I'm good, I'm good. You? Yeah? For who? Expos? That's great. It has been a while. Yeah, I'm sure you can't get away with what we did in Toledo in the Majors. Yeah, I remember that! Hey, quick question, what the hell is a 'Mud Hen?'"

Ansel maneuvered the pickup truck up the winding driveway. Past the 'for sale, reduced' sign. Past the depressed farmhouse with windows broken. Over the gravel. Amanda sat next to him, Daniel on her lap. The former in a cream blouse and light blue jeans, the latter a white baseball tee with blue stripes on the sleeves and his red Ford cap. Keenan squeezed against the door frame, his knees pressed hard together and in an uncomfortable position for his groin. He cursed the uneven dirt and bad shocks, but hope lay ahead as the barn came into view.

Ansel stepped out quickly, his worn work boots hitting the gravel. Another version of plaid over his broad shoulders. Keenan stepped out even quicker, and his glasses slipped down when he landed. He adjusted his blue button-down shirt and bootcut jeans, then pushed his glasses up the bridge of his nose as Daniel ran to the apple trees in the clearing near the barn.

Daniel studied the ground around the trees, apples in different states of decay. Some freshly fallen and hard. Several with brown spots from where worms had burrowed. Most were mushy from skin exposed to the late summer heat. He took a few of the hard ones and threw them into the untilled field.

"See!" Keenan exclaimed proudly, "a ballplayer!"

Daniel tired of throwing the apples and took to the tree and climbed to the lower limbs.

"Daniel," said Ansel, "Daniel, be careful!"

Daniel found a bunch of apples and plucked them from the tree. He inspected the first and threw it down. Same for the second. The third met his requirements and he took a bite. He crunched the fruit as juice dribbled down his chin.

"Should he be eating those?" asked Amanda.

"Ain't worse than what they've been pumping him full a'," responded Ansel. "You got girls, Amanda ... boys eat dirt and bugs, and they're alright."

"Gross."

Daniel climbed down from the tree with pride. He walked to the barn. Inspected its faded façade. The paint peeling in the corners. Walked its length with his hand feeling every aged timber. At its end, he rejoined the adults in the clearing near the parked truck. Keenan and Amanda took in the surroundings steeped in morning light. Ansel nudged the boy, and once he had his attention, motioned to Keenan. Daniel took a step forward, then another and looked up at him.

"Uncle Keenan?"

"What's up, Daniel?"

"I'm sorry," he said as Ansel watched.

"Sorry for what?"

"For bein' mean yesterday."

"Oh, don't worry about it. You weren't feeling well."

"That don't matter, I'm sorry. An' I don't care what a mud hen is."

"It's like a duck, Daniel. A mud hen is like a duck."

Amanda had moved to the barn before the others. Her eyes set on the crooked doors ajar. Sunlight spilled through the opening, through the gaps in the slats. Shadows danced the interior in the back corner where the apple trees swayed in the breeze and filtered the light through leaves and branches and fruit. She slipped sideways through the doors and disappeared. Ansel noticed her absence and turned to the barn, with Keenan and Daniel in tow.

Amanda was crouched down over the freshly dug hole in the barn floor. The two brothers joined her, standing behind and beside. Daniel had no interest in holes and inspected the walls. The missing slats in the roof. Kicked the dirt and took to the loft ladder and climbed. Amanda stood and they all stood in the morning quiet and let the seconds drip to minutes.

"I don't want to be here anymore," said Keenan, thinking he had said it to himself, but with the vocal exclamation he had to make good on his thought. He stepped lightly and behind him Ansel followed, leaving Amanda. She heard Daniel overhead among the hay and took to the ladder.

Daniel was bent over several hay bales, his legs dangling in the air and his upper body hidden between the bales and wall. He pulled himself down and stretched his ankles so his toes could find the floor. He set a stack of yellowed comic books on a solitary hay bale in the center of the loft. He went back, hoisted himself and his legs dangled again. Down again and he picked up a wine bottle, the label faded, then he set it down in favor of a portable transistor radio.

As he set the radio on the hay table, he saw Amanda but didn't acknowledge her. He clicked the knobs and turned the dials on the radio which remained silent. She took a bale from against the wall and pulled it forward, stopping it opposite the bale set with treasure.

"You don't have to leave, you know," he said, still adjusting the radio.

"I think your father wants his bed back," with a comforting tone.

"You don't have to."

She ignored the demand, and her thoughts turned to seeing her husband and children.

"This is a really good hiding spot," he continued.

"It is," as she picked up one of the comic books and leafed through it. "I used to hide up here."

"You did?"

"Yup. Your Uncle Keenan too."

"Did my dad?"

"No. Your dad," she paused and thought how to phrase her words to a young child, "your dad was our protector."

"Like Superman?"

"Just like Superman."

"Who'd you have to hide from?"

"A bad guy."

"Lex Luthor," chimed Daniel, simply to let her know that he knew the relationship.

"A bad guy who, when he got upset, he would get very mean."

"Did he hit you?"

"No, but only because I hid up here."

Amanda put down the comic and walked the length of the loft. She peered out the window and saw her brothers near the pickup smoking cigarettes.

"Does anyone hit you, Daniel?"

"Yeah."

"Who hits you?" as she stared out the window.

"Tommy hit me. It hurt a lot 'cause he's big. So did Michael, but that didn't hurt too much and I wrestled him then we saw a rabbit and chased it but couldn't catch it."

"Has your dad ever hit you?"

"Nah, we just wrestle around."

"Even when he's mad?"

"We don't wrestle when he's mad. Or when I'm feeling bad."

"I mean does he hit you when he's mad."

"Like when I don't listen?"

"Yeah."

"He just yells ... he growls. It's scary."

She turned and walked to the center of the loft.

"C'mon, you ready to get going?"

"Aunt Amanda?"

"Yes?"

"Can I have this radio please?"

"Sure."

"Aunt 'manda? Can I stay with you some time?"

"Of course, sweetie."

Amanda grabbed the ladder and headed down. Daniel followed with radio in hand, and she stood below as he awkwardly grasped for both radio and rung and braced to catch him if his grip was lost. He jumped and sprung from the third rung up and the dirt spread out in fine sediment around his shoes. She put his arm around him, and they left the barn and returned to the teeming sunlight and fettered heat of mid-morning.

Ansel slid into the driver's seat, and Keenan's knees pressed hard against the passenger door. He winced, then accepted. Packed like sardines in a crushed tin box, Ansel turned the ignition and set the transmission to drive. They circled the openness leading to the barn and down the driveway. Amanda craned her neck to keep the farmhouse in view, and it finally disappeared.

Dirt roads stretched for miles as Daniel bounced on Amanda's lap, then turned to pavement for an extent and Daniel fell asleep in her bosom, then dirt again. She too drifted between daydream and exploration of houses and structures in different states. Small dwellings with gardens and American flags set on angles attached to porches. Garden gnomes and children's bicycles leaning against garages. Corner stores stocked with whiskey and beer and cigarettes. Corner stores abandoned with faded signs over boarded windows. A small town holding on—anchored by a hardware store. A McDonald's. Church steeples off the main street.

And in her daydream, their father had called the three children into the living room. The tone of his voice and the whiskey on his breath secreted their mother upstairs to the master bedroom. Keenan had done something, or broken something or not done something, though she could not recall exactly what.

The living room was dark, with only one lamp nearest the window on a wooden table illuminated. Only one light was to be on in any room, and any room unoccupied was to be dark. The children sat on the sofa and stared up at the lanky man, unrecognizable in this rage. Clean shaven with short, jet-black hair cropped. Eggshell white dress shirt, brown belt with brown pants—all seemingly hanging off his reedy frame. Far enough from the lamp to create deep shadows about his form, which exaggerated the whites of his eyes. He paced the length of the sofa, back and forth. Back and forth. He gained momentum in his anger before he spoke.

"Who did it?" he asked deeply, as if his words were in shadow as well.

The children stared ahead, watching him.

"Who did it?"

Silence still.

"So you all wanna be in trouble?"

Again, silence.

"I'm gonna pick one of ya if ya'll don't confess. You wan' that?"

Keenan dug his fingers into his denim covered knees. Amanda's heart raced, but she knew it wouldn't be her if it came to that. She was his favorite and sat in safety, between the two boys. Ansel stayed stone-faced.

"Last chance."

The children remained united. Their father inhaled deeply, then released. He left the room and, in his absence, not a word was spoken. Through the walls they could hear music, as their mother had turned on a radio to further insulate herself. He returned and placed a chair from the kitchen table in the center of the room. He sat down; his legs splayed as he leaned in.

"Am I gonna make the choice?" with fresh whiskey on his breath.

Solidarity still, as Keenan and Ansel knew that even if they both 'got it' it would be a few whacks on their behinds and off to their rooms for the night. That was protocol for such an offense, whatever it was.

The lanky man, their father, stood and exhaled. He looked each child in their eyes and still Ansel remained stoic, Keenan dug his fingers in, and Amanda steadied in favoritism.

And in an instant, he lunged. His bony fingers wrapped around Amanda's slender wrist and yanked her forward as she flew off the sofa. She screamed, and her legs kicked, attempting to find footing on the worn rug beneath. He wrapped his free arm around her, and as he sat, placed her stomach on his lap. He reached underneath and unbuckled his belt, and it whooshed as it came free.

Keenan pressed into the back of the couch. Ansel's breath deepened. Their father's arm raised above her backside and stayed, his veins noticeable even in the dim light. He stared at his target, then, with eyelids slit in rage he looked to the boys.

"I did it!" Ansel screamed above her cries and her pleadings for leniency. "I did it," he repeated as he stood. "I did it," quieter.

His arm was still raised, the shirt sleeve dangling loosely about his thin arm. Finally, his grip lessened against her back until he released. She threw herself to the floor, then crawled toward the hallway.

"Get back here, girl," he said while locking eyes with Ansel. She stayed motionless on all fours, then reluctantly stood and returned to the couch. She restrained herself, yet the tears still flowed.

"Get over here, boy."

As the music from upstairs became louder Ansel walked to his father. Within range, he grabbed the boy and set him over his lap. He looked over at the sofa, and both children hid their eyes.

"If you don't watch it ain't gonna end. You wanna do that to your brother?"

Keenan was the first to uncover his eyes. Amanda followed, and in the dark recess of the sofa the two clasped hands. Their father was satisfied, and he pulled down Ansel's pants and underwear to expose his bare bottom. He folded the belt in half and held the buckle as a handle. He raised slowly, seemingly savoring the moment.

"This is what'll happen when you children don't listen," and he struck down and the leather bit into Ansel's flesh. He let out an involuntary scream, then another as the belt crashed down. After four strikes, he was able to control his reaction. The blows continued, and either due to sloppiness or drunken aim the belt came down and met his bottom. The thin, rough side cut into him, which drew blood that ran down his thigh. He reached his hand back to create a barrier. "Boy, your hand'll hurt too you keep it there!" and his father continued, and the belt cut into his hand which made him remove it. His father's discipline slowed, another whack. Then one more and he picked Ansel off of him. "Pull up your pants," and Ansel bent down and felt the sting coursing through him and redressed, and the blood seeped into his underwear.

Ansel had felt the cracked leather against his bare skin and survived, and from then on, he took it as a badge of honor to protect his younger siblings. To take the physical abuse, for he could not shield them from the psychological. He would stay and endure, while his brother and sister would run to the barn or the tool shed and hide.

Amanda shuddered herself free from the daydream as best she could, stuck between Ansel and Keenan and under Daniel. She turned her head left and looked at her older brother. Eyes set on the road. Expression hidden under that beard; his thoughts draped in secrecy. Memories had molded him, sure, but he did not dwell on them.

Perhaps his history had built in him resilience. Trauma, the beatings and the war and the death had forced introspection from his being. That, to maintain, he had to forgo all feelings, the good and the bad. He had been their protector, their shield from evil, and she felt powerless now as he rebuffed her many advances to protect him now. She wished she could forget, as he, at least on the surface, had. There was never any closure from the past. And no preacher had fully consoled her, comforted her into forgiving or forgetting. She craved finality, the chapter's end that leaves blank space before a new one begins, that would allow her that buffer to heal.

Ansel pulled into the driveway fast and Keenan opened the door before it was completely stopped.

"Jesus Christ!" he said as he stretched out his legs. "Sweet Jesus."

Ansel stepped out of the car and took Daniel from Amanda's outstretched arms. He woke in the transition, and his father set him down.

"Why couldn't I drive?" Keenan asked as he hobbled alongside the others to the front door. "Or Amanda?"

"I wanted to drive," replied Ansel, pushing open the door to the phone ringing. Daniel went to the fridge for a soda. Amanda, the bedroom. Keenan, the kitchen table and a cigarette.

"You gonna answer that?" Keenan asked Ansel as the phone continued to ring.

Ansel lit a cigarette and ignored the question and the telephone.

10

The serpentine belt squealed as the sedan rolled past the motel doors, slowed with brake lights that pushed red onto the vestiges of daylight. The driver stopped and turned the wheel hard to pull into a parking spot. He overshot, set the gears to reverse, and reset his approach. The breaks squeaked, squeaked, and the car lumbered into position. *Click, click, click* into park, and two little girls leapt from the back seat and raced to a door.

"Number nine! I found it daddy!"

Their parents pushed the front doors of the boxy vehicle open simultaneously. The father stood with a groan, the mother with a whisper. He surveyed. The interstate, miles traveled and those remaining. The truck stop, sustenance. The people in the vicinity. Keenan, leaning against the motel wall, one leg lifted with his foot against the brick. Styrofoam cup and cigarette. The two made eye contact, and both stood still. It was easy for Keenan to figure out the man, using whatever vacation days he was allotted in the dearth of summer. Before school resumed for the children. It was harder, then, for the man to figure out Keenan. A traveling salesman? Drifter? Hitchhiker? Child murderer? The man snorted inwardly, then spit on the pavement. Grabbed at his belt and adjusted his jeans under his gut.

"Harold," his wife peeped from the door, "we need the key."

He turned from his dissection of Keenan, pulled a key attached to a luggage tag with "9" written in permanent marker from his pocket, and set to opening the door.

Keenan flicked his cigarette into the parking lot, took a swig of whiskey and spit, trying to hit the smoldering butt. He missed left, thought about another try, but instead opened his motel door and sat down on the bed. He removed his shoes and sat for a moment. Then another. Culminating as he stood up and twisted the knob on the small black and white television on the dresser. The screen flickered, then faded in. He pulled and turned the rabbit ear antenna above the set, succeeding in turning the wavy, distorted image into a pretty weather girl against the backdrop of a map. He turned the volume knob to the right.

"We're looking at a dry evening," she said, "and a dry, hot start to our day tomorrow. Bring your umbrella with you to work though, as a pretty heavy storm front moves in from the west. We could see anything from some showers to thunderstorms in the evening. There's a slight tornado risk, but I don't see anything too serious."

He set his head against the pillow, and his body pressed into the quilt, which depressed the aged springs underneath. The weather girl's words slipped into his subconscious as he imagined how her breasts looked under her dress. How her plump lips would feel against his and imagined them painted red and the dress purple as he stared at the grayscale. His eyes became slits, and he fell asleep wondering how her husband compared to him and what choice she would have made had she known him in courtship.

A semitruck blew its air horn as it departed the truck stop and woke Keenan. It took some time for him to get acclimated. He was in a motel room. It was night. The lights were off, but the open drapes allowed the exterior lights to illuminate the table. His mouth was dry. The television was on. It was 'Moonlighting.' He sat up and put his feet on the floor. Swallowing, he looked at the whiskey cup, the warm beer. He slipped on his loafers, picked up the coins from atop the dresser, and left the room.

The alcove between the office and the rooms contained the motel's self-service amenities. A vending machine replete with potato chips, candy bars, and three types of chewing gum. A vending machine for soda. An ice machine. He deposited coins, and a can of soda clunked through the mechanisms, landing on its side in the opening. He picked it up, pulled back the tab, and the metal clicked. Several gulps, and he walked along the motel doors. A television flicked light in room one. Room two was dark, as was three. He heard the shower through the open window of four, then empty darkness until his door. He turned the door handle, and set it ajar, then closed it without entering. Pivoting, he faced the remaining rooms along the row. Then short, deliberate steps to his neighbor's door.

The drapes were parted several inches and gave Keenan a slim view inside. Candy's silk-covered ass peeked out from under a white robe as she bent slightly and shuffled about the motel dresser. She took out a manila folder, papers haphazard between and jutting out at all angles. She took out a slender shoebox—off-white with 'Kinney's' written in cursive—and she set them on the bed.

At once, he became embarrassed and curious. He turned his back against the brick wall and sipped his cola. Summoned the courage, spun, and knocked softly on her door.

"Go away. I ain't takin' callers right now."

"Um," Keenan started and cleared his throat through the door, "it's your neighbor. Keenan."

He heard nothing for several seconds, then the door opened and tightened against the security chain.

"What do you want?"

"Nothing really," he stammered, "saw your light on and thought you might want company."

"Why'd you think that?"

"I don't know."

"Who are you?"

"Excuse me?"

"Why are you here?"

"Am I not supposed to be here?"

"Any guy runnin' through here's got a family, a wife, and sometimes a couple a kids. Or, he's stayin' just one night and then he's gone. Or, he's a trucker just crossin' the frontage road. You ain't any a those."

"Just visiting family."

"So why aren't you stayin' with them?"

Keenan didn't have an answer, or at least an answer he wanted to share with her.

"You ain't good at readin' people, are you?" as she stared at him through the gap. Keenan didn't respond. "I ain't takin' callers right now," and she shut the door and he heard the click of the deadbolt.

He withdrew and walked slowly to his room. A careful pour of whiskey into the cola can, just enough to dull. One more night in this nothing, he calculated, which had lost its charm twelve hours ago. That's the thing about nostalgia, he reckoned as he lit a cigarette. The smoke rose in the crevasses of light and shadows of the television. It tastes sweet on the tongue from afar, but it will crush you if you stay too long immersed in it. The dreadful memories begin to cannibalize the good with every recollection that becomes fresh as you step into childhood architecture. One more night of unrequested daydreams brought about by sensational cues. One more night, then back east to the real world. To do things that actually matter, with people that actually matter. This time, he thought, he'd do things right. This time, he promised himself he would die trying.

"So, he was bad?" Daniel asked, tucked snuggly in his bed. His thin arms exposed and tinted under tungsten from the table lamp beside him.

"People are both good and bad," Amanda responded, "good people do bad things, and bad people do good things."

"I do bad things when I'm mad."

"See? You're good, but sometimes you do bad things. It's important that you know it's bad and you try not to do it again."

"I get in trouble when I do bad things."

"Well you should try to be good all the time, but I know it's hard."

"Sometimes when it hurts so much, I get mad."

She put her hand on his forehead and rubbed his stubbled head gently from front to back. He turned to his side and tucked his hands under his cheek. She moved her hand down and rubbed his bare back. She felt his spine and prickly ribs. She thought about her children, about holding them tightly soon. About kissing her husband. The college savings accounts she'd set up for them. At home, she felt enveloped in God's grace. At home, life made sense. In this claustrophobia, in what she deemed not much more than a shack, she felt sick. It seemed events just seemed to happen here, and these human figures simply reacted to the good, the evil, or the indescribable. Everything was a cancer to be dealt with only after it was known. The angelic smoothness of Daniel's breaths in slumber. His detachment from family and friends in the sparse overgrowth of rural settlement weighed on her. It reminded her. She felt her anger grow, and she sought a culprit yet found none. She sought an enemy, but found only the lucky and unlucky, and with a kiss on the forehead, she left the boy, flipped the light switch, and closed the bedroom door.

"You need to leave this place," Amanda said as she sat down at the table, not waiting for an invitation from Ansel. "Move to Belleville."

Ansel looked up from the three manila envelopes; the thinner labeled 'Amanda' and 'Keenan,' the thicker 'Ansel.'

"You can get a job there," she continued.

"I can get a job here."

"Where? How long have you been trying?"

"I tol' you, either the Ford plant or get my mechanic's certificate."

"What about Daniel?"

"What about him?"

"What are you going to do? After you pay the hospital and the doctors, what's left?"

"That's why I'm gettin' a job."

"This ain't no place to live," she said, reverting to their childhood vernacular.

"It's away from people, an' it's a fine place to live."

"For you maybe, but what about Daniel?"

"What about him?" he said as he tensed.

"All he does is sit around the house all day, and before I got here this place was a disaster."

"He's fine."

"Is he? He ain't got friends, how's that 'fine'?"

"He's got friends."

She reset herself, not wanting to go down a path in which she lacked information. "You'll be close to us, close to family."

"It's the suburbs, people in your business. Nowhere to jus' be by yourself."

"You're being selfish."

He glared at her, then set down the stack and folded his arms. "You don't know what you're talkin' about."

"Yes, I do."

"You come by here, what, once a year?"

"And you come by us never."

"I do the best for him. For us."

"How many times have I offered to help? Huh? How many times have you just stopped talking on the phone when I bring it up? And now, you don't even answer the phone and the only time I get to talk to you is when you decide to call."

"This is my responsibility. Daniel is my responsibility, and I do everything I can for the boy."

"We ain't kids, Ansel. You can't take this all on yourself. It's killing you. I haven't seen you smile in I don't know how long. I haven't seen you laugh in forever."

"Cause you don't come by but once a year."

"Cause you don't want me here! You don't want anyone here."

"It's cause I'm..."

"Cursed? Cursed, Ansel? You gonna go back to that? You have family that loves you, but you turn us away. Whatever 'curse' there is, it's cause you do it to yourself."

"Look around, Amanda. This place is shit. I can't get a job. I'm alone. The only boy I got is sick. How am I not cursed?"

"You just said you're gonna get a job."

"That's hope, Amanda, and hope is nothing but a dead end. The secon' I get hope, it all falls apart."

"Look," she said, picking up the thick stack with his name on it, "How is this not hope? Tangible, real, hope. It ain't a thought, it's real."

"But why did I have to get beat, and watch my friends die, and lose my woman, and see my son get sick to get here? Why?"

Amanda pushed her back into the chair, abandoning her aggressive posture. "In the Bible there's a story..."

"Don't. Please don't. What God would do something like that to a man?"

"You think you're the only one that's got the short end of the stick? You think you're the only one?"

"It doesn't matter. None of this matters."

In that statement she decided to end her pursuit. She had said her peace and he had said his.

"Promise me, Ansel. Promise you'll think about moving to Belleville."

She set his envelope gingerly on the table, and he took it and held it a few inches above the table.

11

"Can ghost runners steal, Uncle Keenan?" Daniel asked, facing the yard and holding the wiffle bat where he scuffed out the gravel in the driveway to mark home plate.

The sky was clear, and the air was warm. The breeze shuffled the leaves still green but baked on the trees. Through committee, Keenan, Amanda, and Daniel had determined that first base was the tire swing, the top of a discarded pizza box would be second, its bottom cardboard, third.

"No, ghost runners cannot steal," Keenan exclaimed authoritatively from the imaginary pitcher's mound. "That leads to fights and ruined friendships. You get a hit and that 'runner' stays on base, doesn't move until you get another hit."

"When me and Tommy play, ghost runners can steal."

"I thought you hated Tommy?"

"I do."

Keenan waited for elaboration, but none came.

"You wanna steal?"

"I don't know."

"Who do you want to be?"

"What?"

"What ball player do you want to play as?"

Daniel looked blankly at his uncle. "I don't really know any."

"Ever been to a ball game?"

"No."

"Jesus, Ansel! The hell you doin'?"

Ansel stood in the driveway behind Daniel and said nothing.

"Okay, you'll be Ozzie Smith cause you're batting, and I'll be Jack Morris."

"Who's Ozzie Smith?"

"He plays for the Cardinals. He's a shortstop, and Morris' a pitcher for the Tigers."

"Who's better?"

"Well, the Tigers just won the World Series..."

"Jesus, Keenan," Amanda yelled from her position twenty feet behind Keenan. "Are we gonna play or what?"

"Alright, no ghost stealin', you're Smith, I'm Morris," Keenan said, then spit into the grass.

"If you don't feel right, you jus' tell me," Ansel said to Daniel.

"Who's Dad? Who's Aunt Amanda?"

"It doesn't matter 'cuz they ain't batting or pitching."

"Did you hear me son?" Ansel asked.

"Yeah."

"Play ball!" Keenan announced.

Ansel grunted as he squatted in the driveway, taking his position as both catcher and umpire. Keenan got set on the 'mound' and threw to Ansel. Daniel swung hard and stiff, and missed the ball by a good foot.

"Strike one," Ansel deadpanned.

"Alright, Daniel, good try," said Keenan, "try to relax, be nice and smooth."

Keenan wound up and threw the next pitch.

"Strike two," as Ansel caught the ball unimpeded.

"That's alright, that's alright," Keenan reassured. "You got this next one."

Keenan cheated forward and shortened the distance from the mound to home plate. He threw straight down the middle and Daniel swung awkwardly, hitting the ball and causing it to spin backwards over Ansel's head.

"We have contact! That's a foul ball Daniel, so it doesn't count as a strike."

Ansel searched amongst the cars, looking for the ball.

"C'mon, old man!" Keenan yelled, causing Daniel to giggle.

The ball had settled under his truck tire, he bent down and pulled it out and walked back to home plate, tossing the ball to Keenan.

"Bottom of the ninth," Keenan said as he set, "two outs and two strikes on Smith. Jack Morris on the mound." He threw straight again, and Daniel hit the ball, sending it over Keenan's head and into the air. "It's a deep fly ball!" Keenan watched Amanda get under it, then looked back at Daniel, who was standing at home plate. "Run Daniel! Run!" as he pointed to the tire swing. Amanda put her hands up as the ball finished its upward arc and started to descend. She ran in towards Keenan, purposely misjudging the trajectory and the ball landed in the grass behind her. "It's a hit! Can he stretch it to a double?" Amanda picked up the ball and held it. Keenan looked at her, then at Daniel who stood motionless, breathing heavily with his hand on the tire swing. "He's safe at first! And George Brett's batting next!"

"Who's George Brett?" Daniel asked as he walked slowly back to the gravel plate.

"Damnit Ansel! Really? The pine tar incident? You can't turn on a ball game once in a while?"

"Don't get good reception out here."

"Son of a bitch," Keenan muttered to himself. "No reception, boy doesn't know baseball. Don't know Smith, or Morris, or Brett. Bet he don't know DiMaggio, or Gehrig, or Aaron either. I'm gonna kill him."

Amanda laid out a plaid tablecloth on the picnic table in the backyard. Left out in all seasons, the wood was deteriorated, and the bench seats bowed with pressure. She made a note to not have Ansel and Keenan sit on the same side, lest it give and they fall through. The early afternoon heat had settled into sticky humidity. Clouds were unimpressive near the horizon and a breeze blew across the earth every so often, yet enough that she placed a rock at each corner of the table to keep the tablecloth from blowing away.

She had used some of her money to stock the kitchen with food. Canned vegetables and fruit. Sugar cereals. Milk. Frozen orange juice. Bread. Lunch meat, beef, and chicken. Eggs. Cookies. Ansel had insisted on grilling the steaks, but she rebuffed him and set him to boiling the corn cobs. Keenan followed and was relegated to slicing a watermelon and preparing Kool-Aid. Daniel tapped the wiffle bat and watched his aunt from the picnic table as she worked the charcoal barbecue, set out plates and silverware, and playfully scolded her brothers. "Have you ever cut a watermelon before?" "Step one, boil water. Step two, place ears in water. There is no step three Ansel."

"Corn should be grilled," he retorted.

"Not on my watch," and she gave him a quick hug from behind then went back to tending the steaks. Keenan took the oddly shaped watermelon slices and a pitcher of red Kool-Aid to the picnic table, sat down across from Daniel with a beer can and lit a cigarette. He watched Amanda at the barbecue and listened to the fat and grease as it dripped onto the hot briquettes.

"Don't cook mine too long."

She turned her head and gave him a look.

"So, you like baseball?" Keenan asked Daniel.

"Never said I didn't."

"Fair enough."

"Why are you stayin' at a fancy hotel? You don't like us?"

"Of course I like you guys," as he flicked open the beer. "Just not enough room here for all of us to stay."

"You can take my bed an' I'll sleep on the floor."

"Oh, I couldn't do that to you. Why would you want to sleep on the hard floor?"

"So you can stay here."

"Well, I appreciate it, but I have to pack tonight so I can get going early tomorrow.

Besides, I'd have to go back to the hotel to check out anyways."

"Must be far away."

"What's that?"

"The fancy hotel, I ain't never seen a fancy hotel."

"It is," Keenan said unconvincingly, though Daniel didn't register the tone.

"Are you comin' by tomorrow before you leave?"

"Sure will."

"Aunt Amanda is leaving tomorrow too."

"Yup."

"Where'd all that money come from?"

"Excuse me?"

"The big black box."

"You looked in it?"

Daniel broke his eye contact and looked down at his feet.

"Ask your father sometime."

"I ask him all kinds of things, half the time I don't get an answer."

"Tell you what," Keenan said after a long drag, "if he doesn't tell you, I'll tell you about it when you're older."

"Promise?"

"I promise."

Amanda took the steaks off the grill, piled them onto a plate and walked them to the table. She stuck each with a fork and circled the table, leaving a steak at each setting. Ansel walked out of the house with the boiled corn cobs and set the plate down as he sat next to Daniel. He took immediately to cutting up the boy's steak. Amanda took her place next to Keenan and took his hand. He rolled his eyes as he realized the coming words. She reached out across the table and Ansel took hers. Daniel saw this and took both his father's hand and stretched to grab Keenan's.

"Lord, bless this food and grant that we may be thankful for thy mercies be," she recited with eyes closed and head bowed. "Teach us to know by whom we're fed; bless us with Christ, the living bread. Lord, make us thankful for our food, bless us with faith in Jesus' blood; with bread of life our souls supply, that we may live with Christ on high. Amen."

As she waited for "amens" to return, the phone rang. She ignored it, then repeated "amen" with force. "Amen" came from the brother's mouths, with Daniel a second later. Hands released, Ansel continued cutting, Daniel stretched for watermelon, Keenan drank his beer, and Amanda poured Kool-Aid.

"Want me to get the phone, Ansel?" Amanda asked.

"Nah."

"You sure?"

"No one good calls," he responded in a flat tone. "They say it was gonna rain?"

"Said so on the news last night." Keenan answered.

"Looks like they were wrong."

12

The thunder was distant. Flowing. Guttural. Melodic. Far enough that the lightning was veiled. That the stars were vibrant, the moon gave all.

Keenan's motel room was still. Vacant. Dark. His clothes were still sheltered in the dresser or hung with hangers. The dirty ones were piled in his suitcase. Outside, only a few cars sat idle in the parking lot. The truck stop din, too, was muted.

He stared eagerly at Candy's bare ass as it peeked out from under a black teddy. She bent slightly and slid dollar bills into the motel dresser. The transaction gave him the right to stare. To take in her scent. To anticipate what he had imagined before slumber, yet he still stood only a step from the door. The men of the previous nights were still present in his mind, and he struggled to put them out with Styrofoam-filled whiskey. She lit a well-used candle and flicked the match dead. The room was neat, her clothes put away, and no suitcase in sight. The only light, besides the candle, was a dim solitary lamp on the nightstand between the bed and a wall.

"You shower today?" she asked while spritzing perfume around her neck and in the air.

"Yes," he stammered.

She moved smoothly to the bed and crawled seductively from the end to the pillows. She laid open and pulled the teddy down, exposing more of her cleavage. "Well, c'mon cowboy."

Keenan gulped down the remaining whiskey and held the cup against his side. "I, um, I should go."

"Don't you wanna have fun, sugar?" as she slid the teddy up her thighs and revealed tight curls of hair. "Don't you think I'm sexy?"

"I do. I do. It's just..."

She swung her legs off the edge of the bed, walked to him and took the empty cup from his hand and placed it on the small table. She took his hand gently in hers and guided him toward the bed. She sat down on the corner and ran her hand under his shirt and pressed her fingers into him. Traveling down, she curled the fingers beneath his pants, then undid his belt.

"Is it okay if I call you 'Jennifer'?"

She pulled down his pants and white underwear. "You can call me whatever you want, hon."

◆ ◆ ◆

An instance of thunder broke open with a crack and boom. The small home shook from the violent decibel. Amanda shot up from her prone position on the bed, her breath quick with fear and the incoherent thoughts between sleep and consciousness. Lightning flooded through the window, passing easily through the opaque drapes. Her breathing normalized, and she relaxed against the pillow.

She searched the air for her dream as it flitted about and dodged as she attempted to pin it down. The crunching of coffee beans being ground. The breeze through an open window. Basement stairs slathered in invisible glue, she tried to climb but became stuck on the first step. With all her might she pried her foot free. It was a canvas shoe, of which she had in youth. With a stretch she avoided that first step, but the second was sticky too. Again, she tried to free herself, but her shoe came off and melded with the step. She craned her neck and listened as someone upstairs turned the handle on the coffee grinder. The morning light rushed through a window she couldn't see, and from it she felt the breeze, warm and fresh. It funneled down the stairs into the dank recess and wafted her hair. It was God enveloping her. The warmth was so comforting. So serene. So understanding. She lifted her foot again, and as she stretched for the third step, the basement door slammed shut. Dust overtook the air, and she fell backwards. The fear came. She wanted to run. To hide in stowed boxes. Under the tool bench. To press hard against the concrete walls but she was pasted to the floor. Her hands were overcome by a layer of the gelatinous glue, and it expanded as she pulled with her arms but did not release. There were voices beyond the door. A conversation. A man and a woman. Direct and then it became heated. Screams. Still stuck. Something fell or was thrown. The glue became deeper. The screams pulsed in her head and hit such a pitch that her eardrums ached. When she couldn't take it any longer, her vision wavered. The stairs, the walls, the door, they all flew into her, as if she was taking in her surroundings in a vacuum, literally taking them in. The interior of the house caved into her. Then the acres surrounding. A main street with its rows of shops. Then the state, the country and the world flew into her eye and into her head and into nothingness.

In her peripheral, in this infinite cloud of white purgatory, appeared a newborn baby floating in the ethereal. Naked. An umbilical cord to nowhere. He blinked to let her know he was alive, and she watched him float and tried to discern if the levity caused his movements or his own free will. His lips parted and then closed. She smiled, as anyone would, and in response he smiled back, and in a soprano pitch he said confidently, "You." And in an instant, the nothingness spewed out. The world raced outward, resetting and then deeper the country. The state. Main street and its shops. It all returned, and the earthly land was consumed in fire, and the horses burned alive in stables. Automobiles ablaze under overpasses, at urban intersections, and in mall parking lots. Businessmen and businesswomen screamed through broken high-rise windows to fiery firemen who rolled on the pavement. The timbers crackled and fell and turned to ash and smoldered. The concrete cacophony bubbled and split. It was all melting, all returning, deep and hot and unbearable until she was again stuck with glue to the basement floor. At the base of the stairs. And the morning light filtered down and it was God, enveloping her. Comforting her. Loving her.

Another crack of thunder and a pulse of lighting, but no rain. She sat up on the bed and reminded herself. Ansel's bed. Just a storm. Ansel's house. In the morning, leave.

Ansel was right, she thought. He was cursed. She slipped on her shoes and walked down the unlit hallway. In the kitchen she took her jacket off a chair and put it on over her nightgown. She stopped at the couch, Ansel was splayed out, sound asleep and snoring, one leg hanging off. She slowly opened the front door and closed it as quietly. She pulled open her car door and climbed in. The engine whirred to life as lightning lit up the sky. *Click. Click.* The headlights. *Click. Click.* Reverse.

The rain hit the windshield in slow rhythm. *Pop.* A beat. *Pop pop.* A beat. She drove without thought, aimless to the untrained. The non-believers. A steady pace within the country road speed limit. Steady for miles before a stop sign. The rhythm intensified after several miles. At a stop sign she lifted the turn signal. She clicked on the windshield wipers. The thunder boomed, the lightning cracked, and she drove.

Over an amalgam of wet dirt, gravel and rocks. Up the winding driveway. Beyond the darkened farmhouse. The storage shed. And in the clearing before the barn, she pressed on the brakes and shifted into park. The wipers whirred mechanically. The fan, set to defrost, hummed through the vents. The headlights worked to focus the barn walls through the sheets of rain.

He was cursed yet it wasn't his fault; some people are just cursed. Burdened with misfortune and anchored and drawn to despair. It was the responsibility of those blessed to mitigate the doom of the cursed; the duty of those with clean hands and improbable fortune. Those with white picket fences that surrounded healthy children and loving partners. Those whose stories climax with the near miss of disaster, rather than its profundity. It was in their actions that God's will was fulfilled.

Yet as her eyes blurred through the rain and as the thunder coalesced in her ears, she found her Christian beliefs lacking. Not in her belief in them, but in this moment, she could not think of any action she could take. The Indians had their ceremonies. The Catholics, their exorcisms. The Voodoos, their dolls. She felt she had only prayer and song. A repetitive tale that Jesus and God were the ones to act, or the Prophets on their behalf. The followers were to beg for help. For forgiveness. For advice. All her life, she was reactionary, in hiding, in denial. No longer, she thought, as she stepped out of the car and let the warm rain fall upon her head and drench her jacket and her nightgown where exposed.

"Every tree that does not produce good fruit will be cut down and thrown in the fire," she recited aloud and turned from the barn with its sanctuary. She walked past the toolshed where her legs dangled with a doll and she was quizzed on tools. Soaked with rain. Determined. Driven by her own ceremony.

◆ ◆ ◆

The fierce wind blew open the front door, and the thunder that was somewhat muted by the walls broke in. Ansel woke and considered his surroundings. Night. Storm. Couch. He sat up and saw the open door as lightning pulsed beyond the frame. He groaned as he stood, then walked to the entryway and closed the door, pressing against it with his body until he heard a faint click.

The startle had brought him to lucidity, and his drowsiness had gone. He went to the kitchen table and lit a cigarette in the darkness. He was certain he had closed the door and locked it before retiring to the couch. Although, he had also stated they were wrong about the rain so maybe he hadn't locked the door. He went back and forth in his mind until his cigarette burned to the filter and he pressed it out in the ashtray.

Unease led him to check on Daniel, whom he found asleep in bed. Responsibility led him to check on Amanda. In the darkness, even with the lightning, he couldn't tell from the doorway if she was abed. He entered quietly and pressed his hand on the edge of the comforter, then moved his hand inward.

He flipped the light switch in the bathroom, but it remained dark. He flipped it twice more. Nothing. Had she been using the bathroom, he thought, she would have closed the door, and he walked down the hallway to the kitchen. The switch here did nothing.

Out the front windows, he waited for the lightning. It came, but too quick for his eyes to count the cars in the driveway. Again, he waited, and this time the pulse was longer. She had left, he thought but could not conjure a reason.

He sat back down at the kitchen table and set his mind on the situation. Did she simply drive home? In a storm? Without telling him? No. Go for a drive? In a storm? No. Was she kidnapped? Did they know about the money? Who were 'they?' Unlikely.

It was several minutes, or twenty, later that he decided she must've wanted something from their childhood home. But a reason why that couldn't wait until the morning escaped him. He had to go. He had to protect her. Yet he also had to protect Daniel, and by venturing into the storm he was putting him in danger. But did he have to protect her? What if she did go home? What if he drove out to the farm for nothing? No, he thought, he had to go, and he walked to Daniel's bed and stood in silence.

Both doors to the farmhouse were locked, and Amanda pushed up on a window to slide it open. She set both her hands within the frame, pulled herself up, and eased into the house. Her hands found the floor, and she dragged herself inside. The floor was covered with a layer of dust, which stuck to her wet fingers and palms. She rubbed them against her jacket to clean them and stood. The lightning illuminated the unlit room. A plaid couch pressed against a wall. A credenza. Bare walls.

From memory, she found the stairs to the upper level easily; the same steps that creaked in youth creaked now. Even in the sparseness that remained, she felt an identity in each.

In Ansel's room, there was a bare mattress upon a bedframe pushed into the far corner. She opened each dresser drawer and found them empty. A small lamp and scattered pencils were on the desk. Each drawer here was empty. She ran her hand along the painted walls and walked the circumference, then pressed open the closet door. The recess was darker, even with her eyes adjusted, but a bolt lit on the metal clasp of a small box upon a shelf. She reached up, took it down and set it on the bed. She flipped the clasp and opened the box as she sat down. She picked up a t-shirt that was resting at the top and set it aside.

She felt something wrapped as she did. There was a sketch, hand-drawn in pencil. It was detailed and intricate, shadows properly attributed and the likeliness of each accurate.

Keenan hitting a baseball from the view of the third base on-deck circle. He was fully extended, the bat behind him as the ball sailed over the pitcher.

She set it aside and went through each, holding each sketch carefully at the corners.

The back of a soldier as he squatted down. Helmeted, an M16 draped over his shoulder. Another soldier screaming out in pain, prone on the jungle floor. A leg missing and a gash through his abdomen.

A demon, his head exposed as he opened the door to a bedroom. An unknown child cowering under a blanket.

A soldier, dressed down to a tank top as he drank a can of beer and smoked a cigarette. Behind him, a large army helicopter. Behind that, another hovering.

A demon, his head exposed over the top rung of the loft ladder. An unknown child cowering behind a hay bale, his head and hands exposed.

Herself, at about ten years old. Her feet dangling from a branch of the apple tree. She smiled as she released an apple, shown mid-flight, to her brother Keenan down below who extended his arms to catch it.

She ran her fingers over the paper, careful not to smudge the penciled image. A drop fell to the page, but she wouldn't acknowledge if it was a tear or rain water from her wet head.

She set the sketches back in the box without finishing them, then unfurled the t-shirt. There were a handful of medals, but even with the lightning she couldn't make out the small words etched into each. She folded the t-shirt over them and put them back in the box, closed the box and took it with her under her arm.

Next, was her bedroom, empty save for her doll, which lay prone on the floor in a corner. She stood in the doorway and, without entering, felt everything she wanted to feel. She reached in fast and shut the door.

Keenan's room was completely bare, as was the master bedroom. She went down the stairs, into the kitchen, and slumped down on the floor. She felt weight pushing down on her chest. The uncertainty and fear had swelled. It was the emptiness and rawness of being here alone, with no one to delve into the context and counter it with hope. This fear, this rush of blood and exasperated breath had brought her here. She screamed into the nothing and shot up from the floor and pulled open every kitchen drawer. Explored every cabinet. For a solitary match. For a lighter. And the thunder still cracked, and the rain still fell in near solid sheets.

It was an odd sight, Ansel thought. Daniel wrapped tightly in a blanket, laying atop the bench seat in the truck, pressed firmly to the back by the lap belt. The rain was hard, and the wipers struggled to keep the windshield clear. The headlights fought to show the way. Still, he was comforted by his knowledge of the roads. Where flooding was sure to occur. Where dangerous potholes would form in the deluge. He relaxed in the driver's seat and felt at ease by the familiar sound of the engine and the feel of the steering wheel. He drove confidently down dirt roads. Steadily over main routes, smoothly paved.

The corn stalks were high, tended to by corporate-backed farms and the few families that managed to stay above water. The rows continued endlessly and came right up to the edge, with only a small tract of ditched grass separated the growth from the roads.

A slight smile concealed under Ansel's dense beard as the truck idled at a stop sign, surrounded on all sides by the corn. The turn signal clicked. This was his element. The world darkened and mad, screaming uncertainty. He, protector incarnate, rushing into the abyss to ensure safety of those he was tasked with shielding. Steeped in adrenaline, his past failures disappeared into the soft recesses of his mind. Savior. Hero. Patriarch. And when all was said and done, he would deflect praise. Accept all commendations with dignity. With humility.

He pressed on the gas pedal and turned right. The truck accelerated and cruised over the dirt and gravel, and the headlights bounced with every bump. It was the expanse he would miss most when they moved to suburbia. The repetition for miles between homes, between short main streets where the speed limit dropped to nothing. It was a safety issue, sure, but secondary it forced travelers to consider the town. To reminisce about the simpler times, whatever that really meant. The local café. The residents' lives as you peaked into windows at thirty miles per hour. As you counted pickup trucks and American flags. And just as you were about to convince yourself that this here, this was the way to live, the speed limit shifted to forty, then fifty-five, and the town was forgotten.

The car cigarette lighter clicked. The circular metal coils glowed orange at the round tip as Amanda pulled it from the center console insert. She considered the heat as she held the hard plastic in her hand, as the rain danced about the car. She held her hand over to confirm and watched the orange fade, and with it the rain let up. The thunder and the lightning pushed east. She depressed the lighter again, it popped, and she took it in her hand. The orange refreshed, then receded. She would have to run to the house to keep it hot enough to ignite anything. But what was 'anything?' she thought. It would be futile against any wood. She wouldn't reach the upstairs in time. The windows were bare. It would have to be the couch. She would burn the couch, and with it, the house.

She pressed the lighter into the metal casing and waited. Five seconds. Seven and it clicked but she didn't move. She just sat there. In her car. Under the soft rain. What good did ceremony do the Indians? What power does the Pope wield in this world? What magic had Voodoo ever invoked? It was impossible to change the past, and the future was God's plan. It was what she placed her faith on every Sunday. He was infallible. Unalterable. Undeniable.

And what had started in a vivid dream now ended with her laughing aloud in the darkness. Tomorrow, she would leave. Return to her husband and children. These memories refreshed would reaffirm her commitments to her family. To give them all the love she had. To help them. Guide them. And in that moment, she promised her children that they would never know this place, the farmhouse, and the barn, and the apple trees. They would know only love and would never have to cower amongst hay bales or behind shed doors in uncertainty, and silence, and tears.

She turned over the ignition, set the car to 'drive,' and circled the clearing. As she set off down the road, she forced herself to look straight ahead. It was over, and she prayed Ansel would follow her to Belleville.

13

Candy showered. Keenan dressed. Zipped his slacks and looped his belt. A white tank top. He buttoned his olive-green dress shirt, but left it untucked. He slipped on his socks, his shoes, and at the motel door he turned the handle, pulled, then stopped with the door open several inches. He listened to the waterfall in the bathroom and closed the door gently.

He slid the top drawer of the dresser open. He scanned from left to right—a standard white envelope bulged with cash, bras and panties and teddies that he ran his fingers through to feel the silky softness. A slender shoebox from Kinney's atop a manila folder, bent and creased from wear and travel.

With a flick he removed the shoebox top. Photographs developed and photographs instant in Polaroid softness were scattered about the box. Candy, a man, and a young boy posing at Disney World, the Cinderella Castle. A lake, the boy in the sand. In the water. Eating a chicken leg, cross-legged on a beach towel. The boy on a stage, orating as

Abraham Lincoln, the ensemble complete with a construction paper top hat and a fake beard. Posed on a sofa, Candy, the man, and the boy coordinated in Christmas sweaters smiling at the camera.

He replaced the lid and slid the box toward the bras and panties and teddies and flipped open the folder. "May 4, 1985," "Dear Patricia Holmes," "Please remit the total sum owed," "continue to represent you," "appeals process," "$3,175," "James, Coleman, McGuire & Associates." Flip. "In the court of appeals of the state of Iowa. In the matter of the guardianship of Jack G., a Child." Flip. "Eagle Food Centers. As part of this restructure, your position will be eliminated effective Monday, November 19, 1984."

There was a squeak from the bathroom as Candy turned off the water. In the new silence Keenan returned the papers, replaced the box top and set the shoebox on top of the envelope at the right of the dresser and shut the drawer.

A heavy knock at the door startled him and he looked toward the bathroom. Candy relayed no instructions from beyond the door for she assumed he had left. He remained frozen. Another knock.

"Jus' a minute!" she yelled from the bathroom.

In stillness Keenan thought of his options, but there was only one. He walked softly to the door, turned the knob and pulled it open. It was the resemblance to Ansel that caused him to examine the man in the quiet. Deep eyes set further in by the fullness of his beard. The wilds of his hair. Flannel. A bulging stomach. Dirty jeans. Work boots. A sweat-stained ballcap held by the brim in one hand.

In stare, both men accepted the transactional nature of the motel room. Human nature prevailed, and Keenan blushed jealously, and the man asserted his assumed right to conquer through deep nasal breaths and eye contact. Both men were acutely aware that the next move would be for Keenan to leave and him to enter, but it was the physical act that remained in question. The seconds elapsed and neither man flinched. Keenan stood his ground with an advantage; his lust had been satiated and the man still desired relief. He saw a lesser man, with a ball cap in hand, of limited intelligence. He simply had to wait for him to set aside stubbornness and realize his weakness in the moment and step aside. To let Keenan through and his singular desire that quickened while bouncing in the trucker's cab down interstates would be that much closer to reality. But it was Keenan who summoned his own disadvantage, that Candy would be none too pleased if he were still there. That he would be infringing on her business. That his presence was conditional, and he had overstayed their agreement. And in that unspoken realization, the man's desire trumped his trespass, and he stepped aside to let Keenan pass. In quickness he left, walked past his motel door toward the office, and would not return until he knew the man was atop Candy.

"I said jus' a minute, that don't mean you can open the door," Candy scolded the trucker as he stood, hat in hand, within the door frame.

As a witness, the sound of crunching metal is extenuated. It echoes and focuses. For the participants, it's a blip. A microsecond that signals something bad but does not remain. It becomes an infinite buzz beyond the silence that encircles the moment. The mind cannot keep pace with reality. The directional force in flux. The immediacy of death, and the stiffness of a body struggling to deflect.

Ansel never saw the vehicle, nor heard it approach. It had coalesced with the corn stalks, then appeared with violence. The front end struck his door, sent the pickup truck sideways, and the back tires slid out and angled towards the ditch. The passenger side wheels caught and careened the truck airborne and inverted. The headlights lit the road, then the corn, then the sky.

He floated in the cab, only his knees against the bottom of the steering wheel. As a participant, he heard nothing, yet he wholly accepted the situation he now found himself in. He had long ago given up on any semblance of logic pertaining to his curse. All of this was random, and fighting it was futile. Yet in the immediacy of primal fight or flight, he found himself willfully praying, albeit internally.

The truck landed. Inverted. The top of the cab depressed and skidded to the outermost row of corn stalks and stopped. The other vehicle had not flipped and lay on an angle within a ditch. Steam hissed from the radiator. Smoke rose from under the hood. Its turn signal blinked, the headlights lit the corn. Night returned. The rain was soft. The thunder and lightning were moving on. No one made a sound, no one moved.

The rain subsided, and the moon appeared through a break in the clouds, then hid behind new ones, then returned. In the faint hue of lightning afar, a set of high beams came into view. The car approached the intersection at a steady pace, then slowed, then stopped hard. Amanda stepped out of the driver's door and looked at the angled car. Then to the inverted pickup truck. The color. The make. The model. The realization, and then the fear.

"Ansel!" she screamed as she sprinted. "Ansel!" She reached his door and pulled, but the metal had crunched and fused the frame. She roared as she tried, but it would not budge. She crouched down and saw him, his neck bent, and the back of his head pressed hard against the cab ceiling. His back awkward and bowed. She reached through the broken window and checked his pulse, and as her fingers pressed against his neck, she noticed Daniel, his head partially exposed under the blanket. He lay motionless, and in the moonlight, she struggled to detect a breath.

She ran to the passenger door and pulled. It too was mangled, but she bellowed again, and the latch released, and she stumbled back and fell to the ground. It seemed that Daniel was floating, the seatbelt had held and kept him against the seat. She reached over his blanketed body, pressed down hard on the belt latch and he fell into her arms and his eyes shot open in unison with his mouth. She smiled in relief, studied his eyes, and he let out an agonizing scream. Her smile left her as she carried him from the wreckage and he continued to cry out in agony. She held him tight, and through the blanket his ribs moved peculiarly under her fingers. Under the cabin light in her car blood glistened and rolled from his mouth, his teeth stained with redness. She laid him down in the backseat.

"It's going to be alright, Daniel," as she extended the seatbelt over the blanket. "You're going to be alright. Everything, everything's gonna be alright."

She shut the door, ran back to the pickup truck, and thrust her arm through the window. Her heart was racing, her breath was deep, and she could not be sure of a pulse. From the open passenger door, she tried to pull him out, but his left leg was pinned.

"Ansel! Come on! Wake up! I can't open the door!"

One final pull of his arm, and she released and thrust her fists down on the door. "I can't do it Ansel! I can't do it!"

She thought about the other car and ran across the road. She could hear Daniel's screams as she pulled open the door and breathed in heavy bourbon. The bottle had flung forcefully from the passenger seat, shattered against the glove box, and burst open its contents throughout the front seats.

His pale, rotund face glistened sweat and trickled blood. He gurgled unconscious breaths and his neck was turned down, which formed a bulge of fat at his throat, and rolled down to his obese build. An uncooperative comb-over had flung back with the impact and looked peculiar. Amanda saw the shattered glass, a bulge outward in the windshield where his head hit. She extended her left arm and reached for his neck, and the other arm followed.

"Fuck you! Fuck you! Fuck you!" she screamed at him while pressing on his neck, his head nodding violently with every shake and his breaths stuttered and adjusted. Exhausted, she thought she had the energy to slam his door.

"Fuck you!" through the window, and Daniel's screams returned to her consciousness. She ran to her car and sped off, working out her memories of where the nearest hospital was. Her steady hands gripped the steering wheel, wet with the fat drunkard's blood. Her nephew's screams from the backseat. Her reassurances as the car flew over the rural gravel, and potholed pavement filled with rainwater, and on through the darkness.

14

The sun had barely risen as Keenan took comfort in coffee and a cigarette and the Wall Street Journal. Mae's Restaurant was peculiarly quiet, and every mug set down on a coaster was audible. Every plate set down at a booth, an event. He had chosen the counter booth nearest the back, and he wondered about Rhonda the waitress as Katherine refilled his mug.

A woman sat down at the opposite end of the counter. Her hair was pulled back in a ponytail, and she wore a gray hooded sweatshirt and blue jeans. Keenan glanced up at her in curiosity and presumed she was a regular, as Katherine brought her coffee and an ashtray without instruction. The cook nodded to acknowledge her through the kitchen window behind the counter. She smiled, presented a quick wave, then lit a thin cigarette. It was only when she caught one of his glances and locked eyes that he realized who she was. And at that moment, she recognized him and quickly looked away. She took a menu that she knew by heart and studied it. By contrast, Keenan did not look away, and instead grabbed his coffee mug and his newspaper. He stood from his booth and as he walked toward her, she pulled the menu closer. He sat down next to her, and she relegated the menu to the counter and accepted the ensuing encounter.

"I'm here because of a safe deposit box at a bank in Des Moines, Iowa," Keenan said plainly, and without looking at her.

"Excuse me?" Candy asked, looking at him.

"You asked why I'm here. Well I'm here, because of a safe deposit box at a bank in Des Moines, Iowa."

"That's a new one."

"Well, it's true."

"True or not, it really don't matter to me."

Keenan finally looked at her, and she stared at the stacks of plates and the trays of mugs. And she smoked. The cook peeked out behind the window, suspicious of Keenan's intentions.

"I grew up near here, a ways, on a farm," Keenan explained, as he avoided eye contact. "Me and my sister and my brother. My brother still lives here, and my sister lives in Belleville. A while ago, my sister got a letter in the mail from a bank in Des Moines, said that there was a safe deposit box that belonged to our father. Said that he had to make a payment on it. None of us knew about it, and it wasn't mentioned in the will so she got a court order and got access to it about a week ago. There was a letter in it from our father that told us where something was where we grew up, so that's why I'm here."

Candy pushed her spent cigarette into the ashtray. "Why'd they send it to your sister and not your pa?"

"He's passed on. Maybe knew he was close so he put her name and address on it. Was kind of in and out at the end I'm told."

"And your ma?"

"Her too."

Katherine took a plate from the kitchen window and set it in front of Candy. Eggs over easy, hash browns, and wheat toast. Candy pushed the plate toward the back of the counter and put another cigarette between her lips. Keenan took a matchbook and lit the cigarette for her.

"Don't you wanna know what it was?" Keenan asked as he shook the match.

"Don't matter to me," Candy responded curtly, having tired of the conversation and the invasion of her private time by a john.

"Well, anyways," he said as he reclined to reach for his wallet and pay for the coffee, "I'm heading out today. Gonna see my brother and his son. Gonna see my sister before getting on the road." He stood up and folded the newspaper under his arm, then paused behind her, "It's been a pleasure, Candy." She ignored him, and he walked the length of the booths and exited out the door.

Candy set her cigarette in the ashtray, pulled her breakfast close with two fingers and unfurled a napkin which she set on her lap. She shook salt on her eggs and hash browns, then pepper. She organized the fork and butter knife and spoon to the right of the plate. Another puff, another sip and as she contemplated the plate Keenan reappeared, angled off to the side and behind her booth.

"There were also newspaper clippings in the deposit box," as he took in her eyes and faded perfume. "My father was a proud farmer till he got hurt. He was a terrible traveling salesman, but in the end, he was an excellent bank robber."

And he set the Wall Street Journal down on the counter, the center of which bulged. "I hope everything works out for you, Patricia," and he lingered in her eyes, then turned and left. She watched him leave the restaurant, get into his Mercedes, and back out of the parking lot before driving on to the frontage road. Once the car was out of sight, she pulled the newspaper close with two fingers and lifted the pages where the bulge had made an opening. She lowered her eyes to see without anyone else noticing. And she pulled the stacks of bills to the bottom of the newspaper, flipped through them and in tears, she felt something resembling hope.

15

It was the katydids on those hot August evenings that elicited childhood dreams in that suburban America, Their songs in that humidity that never seemed to break. Sleek green that camouflaged against the leaves, with their thin legs and curious eyes.

Daniel watched them from his bedroom window as they clung to the trees. He stared and imagined the view from the bedroom in his father's house, when he was still alive. There was comfort in this new home, but he felt solace with his father too. There was nothing he could do to change anything, and so he watched the katydids.

The evening had settled in. Automobiles pulled into driveways, and men walked to front doors in suits and ties and held briefcases. Women walked in conservative dresses or buttoned blouses and slacks, and each had a purse slung over shoulder.

In one driveway, two young girls sat and ran pieces of colored chalk over the cement.

Each with their own tint of auburn hair. Their own shade of pink t-shirt, their own blue hue of denim shorts. They had drawn a house and a sun and a stick-figure family.

A similarly young boy pushed open the screen door and stepped to the porch. He wore a baseball uniform—a white jersey with 'Giants' in blue cursive lettering, matching white pants to his knees with blue stirrups tucked under his black cleats. His hat an identical blue, with a white 'G' stitched on the front. He held an aluminum baseball bat, and a brown glove was fitted to the bat through an opening in the leather. He stepped to the porch, and his plastic cleats clicked the wood as he bounded down the stairs.

"Good luck, Daniel!" one of the girls yelled to him.

He turned back, smiled, then set off down the sidewalk. He turned down Main Street and walked past the drugstore. The café. The antique shop. Cars slowed at stop signs, then accelerated. He kept walking until he pushed open a glass door and small bells chimed from above.

It was a small office, and near the entrance there were three plush chairs that surrounded a small glass table with several financial magazines strewn about. An oak bookshelf in a corner. A solitary desk made of similarly heavy wood was pushed back near a wood-paneled wall, stacked with papers and folders and a bulky, off-white computer screen.

Daniel sat down on a plush chair facing away from the window and bounced the bat against the tip of his cleats. He listened to the computer keys clack and the grind of data being written to a floppy disk.

"You ready?" Keenan inquired from behind the computer.

Daniel's cleats clicked as he stood. Keenan slid his chair back, and in a pressed shirt and tie and pleated khakis, he bent over and removed his impeccable wingtips and replaced them with Nike sneakers. He rose and grabbed the blue baseball cap with a white 'G' stitched on the front from a coatrack and met his nephew near the entrance. Daniel led the way to the door, and Keenan locked it behind them. Keenan's Mercedes was parked out front along Main Street, and Daniel climbed in, set the bat and glove between his legs, and buckled his seatbelt. Keenan backed out of the spot, and 'Butler Financial Services' disappeared from sight.

Four ball fields dotted the expansive park. Players and parents and coaches arrived. They walked the distance to Field 3. "I'm gonna bat you third today," Keenan said while seeking out their opponent, "think you're ready." He put his arm around Daniel, and they maneuvered through the fence to their assigned bench, which served as a dugout.

"Hey, Coach!" said a young player.

"How you feeling today, Jason? You feel good?"

"Yes, sir!"

Daniel sat down on the bench and took it all in. The gravel infield. The short grass in the outfield. The teenage umpire dusting off home plate. The aluminum cracking against baseballs from the other fields. His teammates. His friends.

Other books by Steven W. Simon

Into the Fracking Fields

The kids in the border town watch the prisoners get off the trains and load up on the bus. Alice has heard the rumors of the people who stayed, their proximity to Nuclear One, their cancerous lumps. Her friend Carmen is driven to see the fracking pad where his father was killed – and Michael, unfortunately, is the only one that can get them there.

Out Pondered the Hare | Poems

A collection of poems written in sobriety. Or a Lorazepam fog. A whiskey-infused detour and lysergic-stamped synapses. All in the hopes that some of this makes sense to those who were not there in those specific instances where there is truth.

1200 Miles from Los Angeles

When his car breaks down on his way to Los Angeles, Sanford takes a job at a small-town diner along the interstate to earn the money he needs to keep going west. He learns that his religion means something different there - for better or worse.

boundharepress.com

www.ingramcontent.com/pod-product-compliance
Lightning Source LLC
Chambersburg PA
CBHW021352150726
47989CB00005B/2221